STEPS
to the
SUN

STEPS

to the

SUN

A HISTORICAL NOVEL BASED ON
THE LIFE OF JOSEPH GODFREY

LINDEN FIELDING

iUniverse

STEPS TO THE SUN
A HISTORICAL NOVEL BASED ON THE LIFE OF JOSEPH GODFREY

iUniverse books may be ordered through booksellers or by contacting:

iUniverse
1663 Liberty Drive
Bloomington, IN 47403
www.iuniverse.com
1-800-Authors (1-800-288-4677)

ISBN: 978-1-4917-8242-2 (sc)
ISBN: 978-1-4917-8243-9 (e)

Library of Congress Control Number: 2015918352

Print information available on the last page.

iUniverse rev. date: 11/20/2015

PREFACE

This book is historical fiction based on actual people and the events of Joseph Godfrey's life. It is not a biography. It is not a documentary. In reading the accounts, journals, and life sketches of those people whom this book is about, I realized these people and events were only part of the story.

There are certain defining points in the lives of Joseph Godfrey and his wives and families that describe his life's trajectory. Of his early life, the dates and sequence of events vary with the source. Some people may understandably disagree with the dates and events depicted in the story. Because of the variations in the accounts, I've purposely been ambiguous in the early timeline of Joseph Godfrey's life. Regardless of the precise order of events, what he and his family accomplished is admirable.

Dates and events are but a fraction of the story. The purpose of this book is to add color and texture to the black-and-white pages of a life story. Just as our individual lives contain many details that flavor our existence, our ancestors also had ideas, feelings, and conversations that enriched their lives and served as glue in their stories.

The fictional thoughts, emotions, and dialogue in this book give a more evolved picture as to how events could have happened.

CHAPTER 1

Joseph was painfully hungry. So was his sister, who whimpered in the corner while Joseph searched the cupboards for the hundredth time for anything edible. Left by themselves while their father worked at the shipyards in Bristol, England, Joseph was charged with doing the laundry, washing the dishes, and sweeping. Never mind there was often nothing in the house to eat. He and his sister, Jemima, often wandered the neighborhood in search of anything edible that neighbors had discarded. At age seven, Joseph was expected to provide for himself and his younger sister.

His father, William, put in twelve-hour days at the yards as a stevedore loading and unloading ships, which in the early 1800s was mostly done by hand. After work, William spent the day's wages at the pub, drinking until midnight. On nights when he didn't pass out immediately upon his return home, he would beat Joseph to vent his anger about his life being so dismal and pathetic.

The children were a burden now that his wife, Margaret, had died. At least that was what he told the children and neighbors—that she had died. After years of enduring his drinking and abuse, Margaret took some of the older children who could work to help provide and left.

She had reasoned the younger children—with the house, beds to sleep in, and money from his job to buy food—would be better off than begging for food and a place to sleep. But William saw Joseph and Jemima as her way of trying to force him to be responsible. Out of resentment, he left his youngest children with no care and little food.

William's daily state had deteriorated to one of two conditions—drunk or wishing he were drunk. He remained sober enough to carry armloads of cargo on or off a ship, but finding the nearest drink was always the first order of business at the end of a workday.

Tonight the hunger pangs jabbed relentlessly in Joseph's belly. Emboldened by the pain, Joseph's search for something to eat widened to the closet in his father's bedroom. There it was, wrapped and sitting on the top shelf behind an old hat—the shape of a loaf of bread. Curiously, Joseph carefully reached up, gently pushed the hat aside, and examined the package. The smell was unmistakable. Bread. Now what? Should they eat some of the bread and risk the wrath of his father? Or should he put the bread back and continue enduring the pains of an empty belly?

An idea flashed through his mind. Maybe, if he was careful, he could slice the loaf in half, scoop out a few mouthfuls for himself and his sister, then put the loaf back together, wrap it up, and put it back in the exact same location. He would even move the hat back to partially obscure the loaf as it did now. He would count on his father being so drunk on his return that he wouldn't notice the missing morsels of bread. Or Joseph could continue his search for something to eat, which meant he and his sister would probably go to bed hungry. Jemima moaned and sobbed in the other room. The smell of the bread made him dizzy.

He made his decision. He had been whipped before. Relieving his hunger pain now would be traded, perhaps, for the pain of being whipped later. He searched the kitchen drawer for the sharpest knife. A dull knife would leave a jagged edge and would be more noticeable. He sliced the loaf down the middle and reached in to pinch a mouthful of the soft, chewy bread. He raised his hand to put it in his mouth but stopped. His sister should have the first taste. He walked over to her as she sat doubled over in a corner. She had not noticed his activity. As he offered her the morsel, she stared up at him. In her eyes was both a question as to where he'd gotten the food and why he was acting so guarded. It was only a split second before the bread disappeared into her mouth. Joseph walked back to the loaf and pinched another bite for himself, then one more bite for her, and one for him. He couldn't risk eating more. He knew the more they ate, the more likely the missing bread would be discovered. He carefully aligned the halves together, rewrapped it tightly, placed the loaf back on the shelf, and slid the old hat a little to partially obscure it. It wasn't much, but the two bites were enough. The children quickly dozed off, forgetting the pains of the day and not worrying what tomorrow may bring.

Indeed, William came home stumbling drunk. He barely made it through the door before collapsing onto a chair, with his head landing on the table in front of him. He spent the night without moving, snoring loudly. Somehow he managed not to fall off the chair. He awoke early the next morning, his head pounding and body screaming with the soreness of sleeping in such an awkward position on hard furniture. He was in a terrible frame of mind. He hadn't eaten solid food since noon yesterday, and he went to find the loaf he remembered he had put on the shelf in his bedroom a couple of days before. The neighbor's wife had given it to him "for the children." He had thanked her and chuckled as he hid it in his closet, realizing it would come in handy some morning just like this one. He had had no thought of sharing with his children. Instead, he had hidden the bread to feed his own belly after a night at the pub.

After a few bites of the bread, William's head was clear enough to notice the loaf had been tampered with. Joseph had not counted on his father examining the loaf while sober. William flew into a rage, grabbed the willow branch he kept next to the door, and headed straight for Joseph. Joseph awoke to the stinging fire of the willow whipping his back. He tried to move away, but his father was wide awake now and followed him wherever he moved. The pain was worse than he had ever experienced. Finally, he was cornered, trapped, and could not escape. He turned his back to his father, who continued to apply lash after lash. The last thing Joseph remembered as he huddled in the corner was his father unloading a mighty reservoir of disgust and self-loathing. Joseph made a promise to himself. He would never again be subjected to such treatment. He would rather starve to death on the streets than endure more of this. *I must run away*, he thought to himself as he blacked out.

As Joseph regained consciousness, he dared not breathe. The beating had stopped, and a small pool of blood had dripped off his back and puddled on the floor. He slowly looked around to discover the house was quiet. His father was gone. His sister sat quivering by the table, trying to understand what had happened. Joseph remembered the promise he had made to himself before he blacked out. He moved quickly, resolutely, ignoring searing pain from the wounds on his back. He grabbed a small bag for himself and gave his sister a sack. He told her to pack. It didn't take long to gather the few items that comprised their personal possessions. He explained to her they were leaving. They could not stay there any longer. He would take Jemima to a neighbor, perhaps the same who had given them the bread. Then he would disappear, never to be in his father's sight again.

Within moments, they were out the door and down the road. Joseph gently but firmly pulled his sister along, helping her to keep his brisk pace. He wanted to put as much distance as possible between them and their house in case their father came back.

As they neared the neighbor's home, Joseph kept repeating to Jemima, "We can no longer stay at our home. Father beats us. I am running away."

As they neared the neighbor's home, he told Jemima, "Knock hard when I get out of sight and not before. Just say what I've been repeating, 'We can no longer stay in our home. Father beats us. Joseph is running away.'"

Joseph left his sister in front of the neighbor's door. He ignored her quiet crying as he quickly walked away. The thought came to his mind, *This is probably the same neighbor that gave us the bread. She'll understand and be kind to her.*

He dared not look around or let up his fast pace. Finally, his strength gave out, and he sat down on a log to catch his breath and reflect on what he had done. He was a boy of seven but had taken action fitting of a man ten years older. He figured he may never see Jemima again, but he knew she was better off. He promised himself he would never see his father again, ever.

CHAPTER 2

As Joseph rested for a few moments on the log, his mind drifted back to a few months earlier. Joseph and Jemima had walked into town, looking for scraps to eat. They had walked down a street with the docks on the side opposite the stores. The enormous ships had made an impression on his young mind. He couldn't imagine anything that big would float. He couldn't take his eyes off them. The sight of the ships had never left his mind.

Now, as he thought about the ships while he caught his breath, a plan came to mind. He would become a stowaway. He would try to sneak aboard a ship and hide till it was out to sea. Surely the ship wouldn't return just to put him off. Even if he were put off at the next port, he would be far away from his father.

With this plan in mind, he felt his strength return and began walking down the road, hoping it was toward the docks.

Just a few moments earlier, he had been walking away from something terrible. Now he was walking toward something better, he hoped. He had no illusions of what he was walking to; he just knew it was toward something different. Though he still may be hungry, starving even, at least there would be no more beatings.

A ways farther down the road, he came to a major intersection. He stood a ways off in the bushes and wondered which way he should go. Shortly, a wagon loaded with coal came down the road. Joseph watched which way it went. Then another wagon loaded with something wrapped in canvas. As it passed, he could see it was butchered mutton. It went the same way as the first wagon. *That's the way I'll go*, he thought. *They must be going to the docks.*

For several hours, he followed the wagons at a respectable distance so the drivers wouldn't notice the small boy following. When they passed a house, Joseph carefully looked it over for any signs of food that had been thrown out. At one home, half a sack of rotten potatoes had been thrown out in the weeds near the road. Even though the potatoes had turned green and a few had sprouted, he found a few mouthfuls good enough to consume. He was careful not to breathe when he took a bite to avoid the foul odor that accompanied the morsels.

Late in the day, he arrived at the docks of Bristol, where fishing boats, cargo ships, and whalers had been docking since the Roman era. In the fading light, Joseph eyed each ship as he walked up and down the docks several times. He sized up each one for the possibility of boarding unnoticed. He also listened to the conversations between the captains or first mates and the crew. Did the captains bark the orders to intimidate and belittle the crew? On one ship in particular, Joseph noticed the captain would often pick up the ropes and show the crew how to handle them or demonstrate a certain knot. The captain always explained the reason for doing something a certain way and the likely results if his directions weren't followed. The crew seemed eager to follow the directions. There seemed to be an atmosphere of mutual respect.

This was it. This was the ship he would board. Being early in the evening, some of the crew were leaving the ship for dinner, and some were drinking onshore before sailing the next day. Joseph thought best to wait until the early morning hours, until the drinking was done and all had returned to the ship and were asleep. Then he would make his move. In the meantime, with several eating and drinking establishments in the area, he would explore their garbage for a little more to eat.

Joseph passed a pub that was exceptionally active with eating and drinking and lots of noise. It made sense their garbage would most likely have lots of leftovers as the diners finished their food and quickly moved onto drinking for the night. What he found in the garbage was a smorgasbord of leftovers for the alley cats and rats. In fact, he found himself in competition with the vermin for several of the bigger pieces. It was poor fare to get full on, but it was more than Joseph had eaten at one time in several months.

After dining at the garbage pile, he moved down the alley to be farther away from the action of the rodents. As the night grew darker, the moon rose higher in the sky. It gave a shadowy, gray picture of his surroundings. Most boys would be terrified to be in an alley, behind a pub, alone at night. But Joseph was strangely calm. Considering he had been living with daily hunger and in fear of his father's anger, this was an improvement. He could melt into the shadows and be alone. At least while alone, there was no fear of a whipping. Was he safe? Probably more so than he had been in a very long time.

The evening breeze picked up, blowing the sounds and smells of the pub toward him. Some loud laughter from inside was followed by the chaotic sounds of a fight breaking out. Someone had been insulted or taken offense, and retaliation ensued. Onlookers joined one side or the other until the whole establishment was thoroughly disrupted, and those not directly affected left to find a quieter pub to spend the evening.

"Drinking makes you stupid!" he said aloud, shaking his head and reaffirming his promise to himself to never take a drink. "Why would anyone intentionally make themselves stupid?"

"But it makes you feel good and forget your problems," he counterargued.

"It may make you forget your problems, but it doesn't solve your problems. They are still there in the morning and are probably worse because of your drinking," he rebutted.

Joseph shook his head in disdain, feeling he had decisively won his argument with himself.

After finding a little to eat and winning his drinking argument, he settled into a nook in the alley behind the pub. He missed his sister and wondered what had happened at the neighbor's where he had left her. He hoped that she would keep the memory of the bread Joseph had shared with her. He regretted that she saw William beating him so violently. She was safe now, away from her father, and perhaps she would become part of a new family.

Underneath Joseph's worry, his decision to leave his sister and run away felt right. He didn't know what lay ahead. He only knew what was behind, a dreaded situation that was worse than death. If his plan to board the ship was successful, there would be time enough to ponder what may lie ahead.

The faintest sliver of light began to show on the eastern horizon. It was the perfect time between the late, staggering, returning sailors and the early risers. Being unfamiliar with ships, Joseph carefully approached the gangplank. After a few steps up the plank, a bolt of fear shot through him. He was unaccustomed to the swaying. The hand ropes for balance were flimsy compared to a lumber handrail. What if he fell into the water? Could he swim? He had splashed and occasionally played in pools in the creek near his home, but this water looked deep. He had never been in deep water. As he hesitated, he thought again of how angry his father had been, out-of-control angry. William always got angry when he was drunk. But at those times, it was easy for Joseph to dodge and slip away, avoiding the full force of his father's wrath.

Don't look down, he thought to himself. *Just stare at the top of the plank and keep putting one foot in front of the other.*

He thought of his mother. He had been so young when he last saw her. He couldn't even picture her face. But he would never forget her arms around him, stroking his hair. It remained one of the last memories he had of her. Shortly after that, she was gone. It was that same love he felt now, urging him up that plank. *One more step. One more step.* One more step, and he would reach the ship. As he stepped onto the ship, it felt as solid as a mountain, even though it constantly swayed in the waves.

He stood on the edge of the deck for a minute or two. He was on a ship! How strange it felt—the salty, humid air, the creaking of the ropes that held the ship to the dock, the popping of the ship's flags in the night breeze. Now to find a place to hide. He couldn't be too picky. Too much roaming around would be risky. At one end of the ship, he noticed a couple dozen large barrels. As he crept closer, he noticed the word "Blubber" scrawled on their sides. Joseph lifted the lid on one of them and found it empty in preparation for sailing, though the smell emitted from the barrel was nearly overwhelming. The barrel was large enough for him to fit in, but could he stand the smell without getting sick? Suddenly, he heard a noise. Someone was climbing the stairs from below. As quietly as possible, he hopped over the edge of the barrel, crouched down a bit, and slid the lid back over the top.

For the first few minutes in the barrel, the smell nauseated him, and he fought hard not to vomit. He found that short, shallow breaths were the best. After a few minutes, he grew accustomed to it, and the nausea left him. He did his best to alleviate the cramping in his legs by shifting his weight from one leg to the other. Pressing his back against the side of the barrel to relieve his legs, the residual blubber soaked through his shirt, and the salty fat seemed to set fire to his wounds. For the next several hours, it was a toss-up which was worse, his cramped legs or the burning wounds on his back.

Finally the curiosity to see what was happening overcame him. He cracked the lid slowly to catch a glimpse of several sailors scurrying about, making the ship ready to depart. A few sailors were hoisting up the gangplank. Others were hauling in ropes.

Despite being fascinated by the sailors' activities, Joseph couldn't ignore the increasing pain in his legs. Without being able to straighten them out, the pain got worse and worse until he moaned. A passing sailor heard him and threw off the lid. The sailor was shocked to see a boy. Joseph had been discovered.

But he was also relieved he could stand up and stretch his legs. The sailor grabbed his arm and jerked him out of the barrel. Without saying a word, the sailor, with the boy in hand, started toward the gangplank.

"No, no, please, don't put me off the ship. My father beats me, and I'm running away. If you put me off, he'll find me, and it will be worse than ever," Joseph begged.

The sailor stopped and looked down at the boy. Seeing Joseph's bloody shirt, the sailor thought there might be some truth to his pleas. Stowaways were a common occurrence. The policy was simply to put them off the ship immediately without argument. But there was something about this situation that gave the sailor pause—the bloody shirt and the concise, clear way Joseph made his argument. "We'll go to the captain," the sailor said, changing direction abruptly and taking such large steps that Joseph was mostly dragged along.

"I found this boy in a blubber barrel, sir," said the sailor as they confronted the captain, who was reviewing some charts.

"Put him ashore, sailor," said the captain without looking up. Joseph repeated exactly what he had said before. "Please, don't put me off the ship. My father beats me, and I'm running away. If you put me off, he'll find me, and it will be worse than ever."

The captain casually looked up. Seeing the bloody shirt, his eyes widened, and his brow wrinkled.

"Take your shirt off, lad," he said. Joseph did as he was told. However, the shirt did not come off easily. The blood and blubber had dried. The shirt was embedded firmly in the scabs. But as directed, Joseph peeled the shirt from his back and ripped open several of the wounds, allowing fresh blood to ooze down his back. It took a lot to shock the captain. He'd had experiences and seen sights that had dulled most of his sensibilities. "You say your father did this?" said the captain.

"Yes, sir," was all Joseph said. It was all he had to say. Captain Fitzgerald was noticeably touched and paused to deliberate the situation for what seemed like an hour.

"What's your name, son?" the captain softly said.

"Joseph, sir." Joseph scarcely dared breathe.

The captain finally said, "You can stay." Then the captain gave the sailor instructions. "Take him below, let him wash up, give him some breakfast, and put him in the bunk near my cabin."

The captain turned away quickly so as not to let the sailor see the emotion welling up in his eyes. *How could a father treat his son that way?* the captain thought. He had never married. He would have liked to, but a sailor's life did not lend itself well to having a wife and family. He often pictured himself as the father figure to some of his sailors. Many of them came from broken homes without a father or even a mother. Perhaps it was this paternal leaning that touched his heart at that moment. He cautioned himself to not dwell on it too much. He'll do the right thing and care for Joseph now, but being bold enough to become a stowaway in the first place meant there was a good chance the boy would jump ship and be gone at the next port.

As Joseph washed up and ate the first warm food in days, it was easy for him to accept the ship as his new home. He made up his mind he would do whatever he could to help out and not be a burden to the captain or crew. He knew nothing about sailing or being a sailor, but he could learn.

He finished his plate of food and offered to wash the plate and utensils. The cook was speechless; no one had ever offered to wash his own dishes before. Just as Joseph was starting to wash, there was a commotion on deck. The cook climbed the stairs, followed by Joseph. As he neared the top of the stairs, the sailor who had discovered him hollered down at him. "It's your father on the shore, calling your name and looking for you!"

Joseph froze, not taking another step. In fact, he felt his feet backtracking slowly down the steps. Would the relief he had been feeling be short-lived? Fortunately, the ship had launched and was several hundred feet away from the shore, making it impossible for his father to snatch him back. Realizing this, Joseph climbed up to the deck. It was easy for him to recognize his father's figure on shore. His heart skipped a beat.

What happened next was seared in Joseph's mind and would be a prized memory for the rest of his life. Captain Fitzgerald was shouting through a megaphone, "This is Captain Fitzgerald of this ship. You, sir, on shore, looking for your son, Joseph. He is with us, and he will stay with us. We have seen the wounds and abuse you have inflicted on him. *You will never see your son again!*"

Joseph saw William duck his head and slink down the nearest alley. The ship continued to gently drift out of the harbor, heading for the North Sea in search of whales.

Joseph went below and found his bunk. With a full belly and a sense of security he had never felt before, Joseph fell into a deep sleep. His sleep was encouraged by the wave motion of the ship, a sensation he had never felt. There was much for the crew to do as they headed out to hunt whales, but most of it was on deck, leaving the area near his bunk relatively quiet.

He was finally aroused from his sleep by eight bells. Joseph had no idea what the bells meant and at first thought they might be some type of alarm. He lay still and listened carefully for any indication of what was happening. A few sailors came below, talking in casual tones until they spied him in his bunk. Even though he was awake, he lay still with his eyes closed, interested in hearing their conversation.

"There he is," one said, "our stowaway." His tone was not one of derision but of curiosity.

"Did you see how beat-up he was?" said the other. "I don't blame him for trying to get away from whoever was doing that to him." With that, they made their way toward the galley.

CHAPTER 3

The first night on the ship brought about a mix of emotions for Joseph. This was the first night of a different life for him. His running away from home was the demarcation between his life on land and his life on the sea. He missed his sister. But he was relieved to be away from his father and all the baggage that included. He had no problem putting it mostly out of his mind. He had little notion as to what lay in front of him. He made the decision to learn all he could about this kind of life. The security of his bunk and thoughts of the kindness of Captain Fitzgerald lulled him to sleep. Still, there were a dozen times he was roused by the strange sounds of creaking masts and wind and the wave motion of the ship. It was nearly morning when he was able to sleep through those things unnoticed.

It was normal for him to rise early and start scrounging for something to eat. Some days he found a piece of a potato, a half-eaten biscuit, or a spoonful of mush. He then cleaned up the dishes and other evidence left the night before of his father being there. He would often go days without seeing his father, as he came home drunk late at night and left early for work the next morning. When they did cross paths, it was rarely pleasant.

Captain Fitzgerald was not like most ship captains. He eschewed vulgar language and chose not to lead by intimidation but by inspiration. His crew reflected this attitude. New crew members either preferred his manner of leadership or soon left the ship in search of a crew more to their liking.

Joseph wanted to be useful. He started looking for simple things to do around the captain's cabin. He straightened some papers, took several coffee cups that had accumulated during the day to the galley and washed them, then polished the captain's boots. Joseph had polished one boot and was starting the next when he reached for the bottle of polish, just as the ship crested a wave and jerked in a different direction. His hand hit the bottle and tipped it over on the desk. He was suddenly terrified. The usual punishment from his father for such an accident would be a whipping and being sent to bed with nothing to eat. Joseph scrambled for a rag and dabbed up the polish as best he could. It still left an unmistakable black stain on the desk. Joseph started to debate with himself whether to go to the captain and fess up or put some sea charts over it and ignore it, hoping to let several days pass before it was discovered.

Just then the door opened, and in walked Captain Fitzgerald, making Joseph's decision for him. He stood there, frozen, with an apologetic look, nodding toward the desk. The captain stopped short, looked surprised, and took in the scene. It took a few seconds for him to see the boots and the bottle of polish and decipher what had happened. Then he looked carefully at Joseph. What happened next made a striking impression on Joseph and the captain. It would drive home the point this was going to be a much different life and a different path from the one he was on just a few days earlier.

Captain Fitzgerald took a step toward Joseph and started to reach out for him. Joseph's reflex was to recoil and stumble backward. The captain, seeing Joseph's panic, put on a big smile, reached out again, and beckoned to him as he slowly and softly said, "It's all right, son. Accidents happen." He then gathered Joseph in and hugged him long and close. That was a unique experience for both of them. Joseph had never been hugged by his father. He barely remembered being hugged by his mother. The captain, even though he often spoke kindly and with tenderness to his sailors, had never hugged one of them. This moment started a new canvas to portray Joseph's life—a painting that would be a measure of all other significant experiences. He was amazed at what he felt. He felt cared for, a new and different emotion. Someone cared for him, not the trivial accident with the polish. That brief incident would galvanize a bond between them that became a governing power in a relationship that would last for decades.

Joseph lay in his bunk that night and thought about the dramatic about-face that had occurred in the last two days, from a terrible, hopeless, repressive, dead-end situation to one of respect and love and opportunity. Even at this young age, he recognized he had felt something—a prodding, a nudge, a determination to take charge of his life. It could have ended up quite badly. But instead, he marveled at the positive turn of events. In the near total blackness, he slipped out of his bunk, fell to his knees, mouthed several words of sincere thanks, shed a few tears of gratitude, and then crawled back under the covers, looking forward to what the next day might bring.

CHAPTER 4

The next morning, Joseph opened his eyes a crack. What he saw was unfamiliar and strange to him. He shot up in bed and jerked his head from one side to the other. He had forgotten where he was, and finding himself in a bunk on the ship was not what he had expected. Memories of the previous few days came flooding back into his mind. He settled down and pulled the covers back over him, reliving the events that had brought him there. He heard few sounds other than the creaking of the ship, the wind in the sails, and the occasional footsteps of one of the sailors going about his early morning duties up on deck. He progressed to being fully awake about the time he heard, "Joseph, how'd you sleep?" It was Captain Fitzgerald coming out of his cabin.

"It was all right, I guess. It was a bit strange for me," Joseph replied.

"You'll get used to the sea in a few days," the captain softly replied. "Before long, it'll be solid ground that'll seem strange."

Both of them respected this new situation, gauging each comment and reply thoughtfully so as not to offend while expressing respect for each other properly. In the back of the captain's mind was the small, persistent thought that this could be the beginning of a father/son-type relationship he had never had but longed for deep in his soul. The only adult relationship Joseph had known was one of intimidation, brutality, and coarseness. He also longed for a stable relationship of mutual respect and, dare he think, love.

After some breakfast, Joseph and the captain went on a tour of the ship, all the decks, top to bottom. He met many of the crew, who seemed to take their cue from the captain on how to treat this stowaway.

A stowaway had never been allowed before. This time was different. For some reason, the captain quickly developed an affinity for Joseph. Here was a young mind, eager to learn. And the captain had several decades of knowledge he was anxious to share. There was a kinship, a familiarity between them that neither could explain but was definitely felt.

Joseph was awarded the position of cabin boy. The captain explained there would be no freeloaders on the ship. Joseph's duties were mainly to serve the captain but could be expanded to any of the crew with permission of the captain. The list could be boiled down to one all-encompassing rule: do what the captain wants you to do and not what he doesn't want you to do.

An illustration of that rule came about shortly after the voyage started when Joseph decided he would help out by straightening the captain's desk. When the captain went looking for a certain chart and found it wasn't exactly where he had left it, Joseph learned what you don't do is just as important as what you do. After several decades of the captain arranging, straightening, organizing, and rearranging his desk, he was not used to someone else being involved. But he was grateful for Joseph's help, including making his bunk, hanging up his clothes, and getting his cup of coffee from the galley when he got up in the morning. And he enjoyed a new face at his table at dinner. The first mate and harpooners, who were occasionally invited to eat with the captain, had heard his stories at least a dozen times, and Joseph was a fresh pair of ears.

For now, Joseph would work at becoming a whaler. He would work at every position, starting with just watching and standing near the captain, staying out of the way. "Well, what did you think, son?" asked the captain after a particularly smooth launch and the boat was off chasing the whale.

"That was a good launch, sir." The captain had began calling Joseph "son" not as a term meant to be taken literally but to put some differentiation between Joseph and a crew member, where the captain always used the term "sailor." But Joseph always referred to the captain as "sir" to show he respected him and didn't expect treatment different from one of the crew. "I'm always surprised how men of such different

17

types work together, even expecting how each other will move," Joseph continued.

It was more than five years before the captain would let him accompany a launch after a whale that had been spotted, and then only in the calmest of seas and under the strictest instruction that he was not to participate in any way in the activities. Eventually, he tried harpooning a couple of times but found he just didn't have the killer instinct necessary to be successful. Harpooners had to have a do-or-die mentality. In addition to great athletic ability, timing, skill, a good sense of balance, precise muscle coordination, good eyesight, and concentration, they needed to be able to anticipate what the whale would do at any given moment. Many harpooners were fugitives—bold, fearless, and running from the law. Others were natives from Africa or a South Sea island who were raised with the "kill or be killed" creed.

As he grew and gained weight and strength, he helped launch the boats when a whale was sighted. He also put in countless hours at the try-pots cooking the blubber into oil. It wasn't until he was an adult in his early twenties he was allowed to help row as they chased the whales. This was one of the most dangerous jobs and could result in injury or drowning. It also required the strongest men with the most stamina. The chase often took hours, and the men rowed for miles before they gave up or were successful in killing a whale. Just as dangerous was the job of stripping and gutting the whale. Handling a razor-sharp knife while balancing on a carcass with the wave action of even a calm sea and the ever-present sharks prowling around was not a position Joseph sought after. He did enjoy the freedom, openness, clean air, and consistency of the lifestyle.

He and Captain Fitzgerald had a special bond, and he enjoyed most of the rest of his family of sailors as well. There were always a few that were contrary and tended to be bullies to build a pecking order. More than once, the captain stepped in to correct a situation. And if it didn't improve, the offending bully was put off the ship at the next available stop. It only took once for the ship to make an unscheduled stop in a foreign country to get rid of a hardhead; that left a lasting impression on the rest of the crew.

CHAPTER 5

Whaling in the early nineteenth century was vital and dangerous. It provided valuable oil for lighting and the lubrication of machinery in the budding industrial revolution. The industry attracted men who were daring, adventurous, and preferred the isolation of the seas to the crowding of the cities. The men were often escaping their past and found this as a way to start a new life. Many lives were lost in the industry. And compared to working in the mines, where there were also many lives lost and health was destroyed, the risks were accepted. There were a couple of mines near Bristol, but most of the English mines were in the north end of the country. At least on a whaling vessel, one could see the sun, experience the wind and rain, and have his abilities challenged.

Unlike merchant ships, the profitability of a whaling voyage, which could last for several years, was shared with the crew. When a new man was hired, the fraction of the profits he would take was negotiated. It depended heavily on his experience and abilities. A new, inexperienced man may only make $1/500^{th}$ share. A harpooner may make $1/75^{th}$. The captain, owners of the ship, and financiers could take up to one-fifth. Some successful voyages would make a tidy profit, and word would spread fast in the pubs and churches, bringing a new crop of men applying for the next voyage. However, some voyages would only provide food to eat and a place to sleep for the sailors. With whale oil in barrels in the hold, which was tradable all over the world, they could stop at ports along the way and barter for the supplies they needed. The world was their grocery store. Depending on what part of the world they were in, they could get rice, wheat flour, beans, beef, poultry, salt, and other spices. In most ports, they could obtain rope and sail repair materials. And of course, fish was always on the menu. The goal was to obtain more whale oil than was required to trade for supplies, and that was the basic reason most voyages were not months long but years long. There was no need to return to their home port until the hold was full of oil, spermaceti, and bone. Their life was the ship. And as long as they killed more than they consumed, they could go a long time without seeing their home port.

Traveling all over the world, the ship became a sort of a traveling trading post, taking spices, foods, and materials from one region and then sailing to an entirely different region where the commodities were uncommon and in high demand, trading them at a good profit. Sometimes the ship came home as successful in trading commodities as in hunting whales.

Sometimes weeks were spent in intense boredom when the weather was fair and they saw no whales. The boredom was punctuated by periods of crazy excitement and activity when a pod of whales was sighted. Several rowboats were launched to give chase in hopes that one of the harpooners would find his mark. At times they would row for miles, kill one or more whales, and then row to meet back up with the ship, whales in tow. The kill was followed by a period of round-the-clock dressing of the whales, cutting strips of blubber and rendering or cooking it in large pots called try-pots to convert it into oil, which was stored in barrels and placed in the lowest hold of the ship. The dead whale was tied alongside the ship while the "cutting in" or "flensing" took place. One or two men balanced on the whale carcass, cutting the strips. Hoists with ropes and pulleys would lift the strips of blubber onto the ship and down to the try-pots, which were on a lower deck. This part of the work was exhausting and bloody. Sharks were a constant menace while cutting up a whale. Often a sailor would be assigned to stand watch and be ready to throw a rope to a sailor who had slipped off the whale carcass. It was a life-and-death race to get him out of the water.

Not only was the blubber harvested, but many of the bones were as well. Whalebone had a hundred uses, from needles to staves on corsets. Another substance harvested from sperm whales was the spermaceti, a waxy substance contained in the head. It had no taste or smell but was very useful for candles, lubricants, cosmetics, and medicines. There could be several hundred gallons of the substance in one whale head.

As the whale population diminished, crude oil, which had been around for thousands of years, was starting to be refined into kerosene, and later into hundreds of other fuels, lubricants, and medicines. Commercial drilling also greatly expanded the availability of crude oil. Before drilling, tar pits and surface pools were the only source of crude oil.

CHAPTER 6

"Thar she blows!" was the signal that set off a flurry of events aboard the ship. She had sailed mostly north, approaching the Arctic Circle. Being summer, it was strange to not see the sun set until nearly midnight, and then after a few hours of twilight, to see daylight approaching. Sleeping during such hours took several weeks for Joseph to get used to. With so much daylight, the whale watch lasted over twenty hours a day.

Joseph's heart beat faster as the sailors scurried to assemble and launch several boats to pursue the whales. He was careful to stand out of the way and observe closely what took place and in what order. Captain Fitzgerald was also watching closely for details. Some details were unnoticed by Joseph, such as who hadn't learned their assignments, who seemed to be in the way of another operation, and who was slacking. Getting the chase boats launched quickly with the right gear and men was often the difference between getting a shot at a whale and missing the opportunity.

The captain could send out as many as four boats, but this left the ship short of enough crew to sail efficiently. Sending out more than two boats stretched the abilities of the harpooners. The captain had two seasoned harpooners in his crew. Thus, two boats were launched most of the time. He also had three others he considered "in training" or second-stringers. He would only send out the third and fourth boats if a good-sized pod were sighted.

This time, two boats were launched. The watchman indicated he thought there were only two whales. Joseph was intrigued by the whole operation. Watching a team operate together to achieve a goal was impressive. Captain Fitzgerald played a key role in establishing the attitude of the crew. He knew that attitude made the difference between a successful voyage and one that just paid expenses. It also was a key factor in the difference between enjoying what you were doing and simply tolerating life. Brisk discussion was encouraged, but at the first clenched fist, the captain stepped in. He stood in the middle of the group, calmly looking each man in the eye, and explained why they were important to the ship and why they were different. Each man had his unique strengths. These were often the first positive compliments some men had heard in their lifetime. He then explained what conduct would be expected. Those who couldn't comply didn't last long on the crew, often leaving at some foreign port and signing on with some other ship more in line with their demeanor. There was always a certain amount of crew shuffling at the port cities. People are most comfortable with those like themselves.

Muscles screamed with pain as the men put all their strength into the oars. After several weeks of tidying the ship and doing menial chores to keep busy, the jolt of this sudden excursion and excitement would push the men to their limit. Several of the men would become so exhausted they would puke over the side, wipe their mouth, take a swig of water, and resume rowing. Later in the voyage, after many launches and miles and miles of rowing, their stamina would double, and they would be able to row at top speed for several hours.

The captain was following the action with his telescope, constantly muttering comments and directions as if the crew could hear him. Joseph could tell they were getting close to taking a shot. The captain's voice grew louder with more excitement. "Not yet ... not yet ... not yet ... *now!*" A few seconds elapsed as the world stopped spinning, and no one breathed. Did the harpoon find its mark? Whales instinctively dive when they feel the harpoon, whether a glancing blow or one that sinks deep inside to find some vital organs. Each second that ticked by reduced the possibility that the whale had been hit. After an eternity, actually only seven or eight seconds, the captain sighed and mumbled a few words that Joseph had never heard. They weren't the common swear words he's heard his father yell but some combination of seaman's language and perhaps a few foreign words the captain had picked up over the years. Sailors are known for their bad language. But while these were unmistakably words of frustration and disgust, they were not swear words. This struck Joseph. In fact, he realized the whole time he'd been on the ship, he had not heard the captain swear at all. Most of the crew did but not Captain Fitzgerald. At this moment, Joseph's admiration for the captain grew a giant step. He'd already been impressed at how the captain related to the men, not using threats or intimidation but leading by example trying to inspire them to improve.

This first harpoon had missed its mark. The whale had gone deep, and even though the crew would continue to watch carefully for thirty minutes or more for another shot, they would not get another.

The captain turned his attention to the other boat, which was farther away in a different direction. From his muttering, Joseph decided the other boat must be mounting a good chase and was closing in. Again the volume of his voice gradually grew over several minutes as the distance between the whale and boat decreased. Now his voice was not a whisper but a yell. "Just about … just about … a little more … more … *now!*" Again, all life was suspended while they watched for any sign that the whale had been hit. Without a spyglass, Joseph could barely see the boat with the crew. But there was no mistake when he saw the men all leap to their feet in unison and the captain let out a cheer. Now he could see a bright red telltale streak of blood appearing on the water. The harpooner readied another harpoon to finish off the whale when he came near the surface. Again, another cheer from the captain as the second harpoon was thrown. A few minutes later, the whale floated to the surface, and the crew, energized by their success, began rowing back toward the ship, whale in tow. The captain gave directions to steer the ship to meet them.

Daylight was fading fast as the whale was tied alongside. Ropes and pulleys, lanterns, knives, and trays were all readied. A fire was started at the try-pots to begin the melting of the first strips of blubber into oil as soon as they were taken from the carcass. Everyone was to work through the night and for most of the next day to secure all the products. Besides the blubber, the next most valuable product was the spermaceti, then some of the bones. The liver was always harvested, cooked up, and eaten by all on board, not only to add some variety and something fresh to their diet but as a celebration of the kill. When Joseph was offered some, he took a deep breath, cut off a marble-sized piece, closed his eyes, tried not to breathe, and popped it in his mouth. He started chewing, then decided against chewing and swallowed it in one piece, followed quickly by a large swig of water. He tried not to wince as the crew cheered. Whale liver was certainly an acquired taste. It would be several years before he could put a slice on his plate and get it eaten without a fuss.

CHAPTER 7

Seven years had passed since Joseph had hidden in the barrel. The ship was making its way back to Bristol to unload, restock, and settle up with the owners. They also needed to acquire a few new crew members to replace some that were leaving and a couple who had jumped ship in a foreign port after becoming entangled in a questionable situation, usually gambling debts or a woman. The ship had been back at their home port several times since Joseph had crept aboard. Each time, Joseph's stomach had stayed in knots. He never left the ship, even stayed below deck most of the time. But he also knew that would have to change. He decided this time he would at least leave the ship but stay near the docks.

Joseph was having mixed emotions as land was sighted, and he realized he was only a few hours from where his father lived. There was the thrill of seeing his homeland, mixed with the dread of running into his father. He knew the chance of that happening was slim at best. But any chance was too much as far as he was concerned. He rehearsed what he would do in his mind. If he happened to meet up with his father, he would immediately make a beeline for the ship. With his longer legs and much better physical condition, he was confident he could outrun his father. Once on the ship, even if his father followed, Captain Fitzgerald and crew would immediately throw him off in such a way as to ensure he would not try to reboard.

It was late in the day when the ship was secure. The unloading would begin in earnest the next day. Most of the crew was anxious to go ashore and find some local food and drink. Not Joseph. Even though he was still too young to drink, one of his absolute, rock-solid promises to himself was never to take even one drink of alcohol. Whenever he thought about drinking, the horrible sight of his father towering over him with switch raised above his head, face in a contorted rage, flooded into his mind.

The next morning, Joseph convinced himself it was time he set foot in his home port again. He left the ship and went to a pub for breakfast. It had been a long time since he had been able to enjoy a glass of milk and some fresh bacon and eggs. He then decided to venture to a nearby shop and see what had changed since he had been there last. He stopped in a rigging shop that catered to the ships and had tools for the farmers and miners around town. He had gained a new appreciation for tools and ropes and enjoyed browsing through the items. While looking at some shovels and rakes to be used on the farms, he caught a glimpse out of the corner of his eye that sent chills through his body. He froze and then ever so slightly turned his head enough to get a good second look. It was his father. He appeared to be after some gloves or something he might use in his work. Scarcely daring to breathe, he watched. As his father moved to the left of the store, Joseph moved to the right. As his father moved toward the back of the store, Joseph moved to the front. He ducked behind a stack of buckets and baskets as he moved closer to the door. Once through the door, he let out the breath he'd been holding in and headed down the street, around the corner, and back to the ship.

He immediately went below to his bunk and sat down to regain some calm. The memory of the beatings, the hunger, the bread, running away, hiding on the ship in the barrel, being discovered, and Captain Fitzgerald shouting to his father, "You'll never see your son again," all played out in his head. In fact, his father hadn't seen his son, but the son had seen the father. The captain, in his office preparing to go settle up with the owners, noticed him and was curious why he was back so soon. When Joseph looked up to answer, the captain noticed he was out of breath, trembling, and white as a sheet. Alarmed, the captain walked over, sat on the bunk next to him, and said, "What happened?"

Joseph blurted out the events of the morning. The captain put his arm around Joseph and pulled him close. He could feel Joseph shaking as his shallow breathing gradually became more normal and the tenseness in his shoulders relaxed. "If you want to leave the ship again before we sail, I'll go with you," said the captain.

Joseph stayed on the ship the rest of the time they were in Bristol, except when the captain announced to Joseph he was going to pick up some personal items in town and asked Joseph if he would like to go. Joseph wasn't eager to leave the ship, but he realized he needed to face his fear, and this would be a way to prove to himself he could. Like the first time he ate the whale liver, he knew he needed to do this, even though he dreaded it. He learned to repeat over and over in his mind, "I don't want to do it, but I need to do it. So, I'm going to do it." This little trick would help him accomplish many things in his life, things that were unimaginable to him at this point.

The next day, Captain Fitzgerald told Joseph he was going to meet with the owners of the ship and would be gone several hours. The captain returned from his meeting with the owners in a very good mood. It had gone well, and the owners were pleased. When he approached the gangplank, he was carrying several sacks that were quite heavy. He stopped on the dock and called up to have Joseph come down to help carry the bags up to his office. The captain's good mood spread through the crew like wildfire, and everyone was laughing and joking with each other. They carried the bags into the captain's office and set them on the floor. Then he told Joseph he needed some time to sort things out, and Joseph was to remain outside his door for the duration. He was not to let anyone come in or disturb him. This was the only time since he had been on the ship that he had seen the door to the captain's office shut. Normally his door was always open to receive any who came to see him.

Joseph sat on his bunk, puzzling over what was going on. It wasn't bad, or else everyone wouldn't be so jovial. Perhaps some reassignment of duties, Joseph thought. The first mate and a harpooner approached. Joseph stood and told them that the captain had asked not to be disturbed. After a few thoughtful moments, they simply nodded and walked away.

After nearly two hours, the captain emerged and asked Joseph to go get one of the last crew member who had joined the ship. When he arrived, he and the captain went into his office and shut the door. After a few minutes, the door opened, and the man emerged carrying a small bag but with a big smile on his face. He nodded to Joseph and left. The captain then asked to see another crew member. Joseph complied. This happened over and over. Joseph realized he was meeting with every member of the crew. He had never seen this before. When the harpooners and the first mate emerged, they were not carrying a bag but a small chest. As each man left the office, they gave a big nod toward Joseph. It was almost a bow. Now Joseph was really puzzled.

After the first mate left, the captain asked Joseph to come in. He entered, and the captain shut the door and motioned for Joseph to sit down next to his desk. Joseph felt some pangs of fear well up inside him, but he quickly put them aside, thinking how pleasant everyone had been as they exited. Even the harpooners, who were some of the most cranky and ornery men he'd ever seen, were smiling when they left.

"Here's your cut," said the captain with a smile, nodding at a bag on the table. Joseph was still puzzled.

"My cut?" he said as he leaned forward, trying to understand what was happening.

"Your cut of the profits—you know, the money."

Joseph was stunned. Captain Fitzgerald was paying him? Wasn't it enough that he fed him, provided a place to sleep, clothes when he needed it, and taught him how to be a whaler? Whatever amount was in the bag didn't matter. What mattered was he had been paid. He had some money of his own. He had never owned even one coin before. What should he do with it? What would he buy? Could he get some of it to Jemima? He hadn't tried to contact her for fear that would raise the chances of a run-in with his father.

The captain could see that, now that Joseph had means, he was overwhelmed. The captain chuckled and said, "If you like, you can keep it here in my office. And whenever you want some of it, I'll get it for you." Joseph let out a sigh of relief as he jumped at the offer. This changed everything, mostly his attitude and opinion of himself. He had value. The young boy that had managed to gather enough grit to leave his abusive father and had felt of little worth to anyone now had value. He found himself thinking of how he could do an even better job as a whaler. How could he be of more value to the captain and the crew? He liked this feeling of self-worth. Everything looked a little brighter. He was now a teenager and had most of his life before him. He had thoughts of the future and what he might accomplish.

CHAPTER 8

The ship traveled to hunt in the North Sea in the late spring, even venturing into the Arctic Circle a few times during the few brief weeks of summer that allowed safe, non-iceberg-infested sailing. As the weather grew colder, they would migrate south around the Cape of Good Hope of Africa. However, one year they sailed around Cape Horn of South America and then went near Australia, the Philippines, and Hong Kong. As the weather got cold in the Southern Hemisphere, they continued north near Japan and Korea.

For a boy who was still a teenager, this was heady stuff. Very few could boast of seeing most every region, climate, and culture of the world, especially at a time when world travel was so new and rare. Not much time was spent at these ports. The biggest deterrent to a lengthy stay was the language. Most communication was done by a combination of hand gestures, facial expressions, and body language. That seemed to be enough for them to acquire the supplies they needed. The whale oil they offered as barter was the best, most common currency they could have. The world used the oil for lighting, heating, and medicine, and the bones for tools.

At a stop at Hong Kong, the ship needed extensive repair materials for one of the sails, and they were running low on fabric and rope. Their flour was low, and they hoped to pick up a supply of rice. Joseph was surprised to hear many of the residents speak English. Even though it wasn't a British territory yet, trade had expanded greatly, and many Brits lived there. For this reason, Captain Fitzgerald felt a kinship with Hong Kong, and the stay extended for several days beyond what was usual.

This stop was also when Joseph became aware of how most sailors acted when in port. After some sightseeing, he was content to stay on the ship while most of the crew left the ship, not returning untill early morning. After dinner at a local eatery, the captain usually returned and spent the evening on the ship. At night, he and Joseph would spend hours talking about life and many of the whaling events the captain experienced before Joseph came aboard.

It was during these late-night sessions that Joseph heard the thoughts and feelings of a wise man who had seriously considered who he was and the reasons for him being who he was. What Joseph heard helped him formulate an approach to life that stuck with him. He learned that Captain Fitzgerald was quite religious and would often pray, in his way, while alone at the wheel or in his cabin. He hungered for family but settled for considering the crew his family. At the same time, he remained distant enough to be an effective captain and role model. He had allowed himself to get closer to Joseph than he had any other person on the ship. Joseph reciprocated by pointing out that the captain was the only father and role model he'd had. The abuse and degradation he suffered at his home had forever severed any family ties there, except for his sister.

He had other siblings that were sent away to distant relatives after his mother died, or so he had been told. Now that he was older, he began to realize that the siblings left at the same time he was told his mother had died. It came into focus. His mother had not died as his father had said. She had left and taken some of the children. And he knew why she left. The father's drinking and abuse had broken the family, and she left to survive. The same reason Joseph left. As soon as this thought settled in his mind, another bigger thought blasted into his mind. *My mother might still be alive!* Immediately he felt compelled to look for her. But he was now on the other side of the world. And even if he were near Bristol, where would he start looking? The only place he could start would be to question his father. That meant he would have to face him. Two completely opposed thoughts were battling in his mind; he would love to find his mother, but he would hate to face his father. Joseph couldn't handle those two opposite emotions at the same time.

He couldn't hold these thoughts in. They came spilling out while he was there with Captain Fitzgerald. The captain wisely just listened carefully, nodding his understanding. Being so far away, it would be at least a year until they were in Bristol again, so he left this dilemma open for now.

Joseph often wondered about his family members and if he would ever see them again. He was anxious to tell them of his adventures. He considered his life a good life and wished the same for his family. He was content, at least for now, to concentrate on his whaling duties and would think about his family in the future should circumstances present themselves.

CHAPTER 9

Thoughts of his mother still being alive and the welfare of Jemima were persistent, especially when he was in the crow's nest on watch for whales. Being high above the deck, he was away from the noise and commotion of the sailors carrying out their duties. It was quiet except for the rustle of the breeze and rhythmic surging of the waves against the ship's hull. A watch lasted six hours. Six hours with generally no interaction with anyone. It gave plenty of time to ponder. There was time to turn a question over and over in his mind—to examine it from every possible angle and to consider the pros and cons of each option.

The captain had announced, just today, a change in course, which would direct them toward Bristol, their home port. It would still be ten days or longer before they arrived, but it brought the thought of his mother and sister to the forefront. Should he try to find them while he was there?

The desire to find them was as strong as ever, to find out where they were and how they were doing if he could. *But what about running into my father?* was always the next question that followed.

He was older now, in his twenties. *Jemima would be in her late teens, perhaps married. I could even be an uncle.* The arguments on the plus side were racing through his mind. *Perhaps she has seen Mother and knows where she is. I could start looking at the house where I left Jemima when we ran away.* Then the negative side of the argument started playing. *Where I left Jemima was only half a mile from my father's house. That is too close for comfort. I don't want to risk running into him, or if he learned I was in the area, he might start looking for me.* The thought made Joseph visibly shudder. As he shuddered, he thought, *It's a good thing I'm up here in the nest. The crew would think I was going crazy.* Then another thought came to him. *What's the worst he could do? What is the worse that could happen? I'm a man and much tougher than before. He couldn't hurt me physically. He could spout off with a string of swear words or threaten me or taunt me for running away. But those are just words and will only do damage if I let them. I'm in control of how they affect me.*

As the days passed and they came closer to Bristol, Joseph was determined to make an effort to find his sister and find out what he could about his mother. He was drawn to the thought of a meeting with his sister. At the same time, he got a knot in his stomach at the thought of even being in his old neighborhood, with a chance of meeting his father. It made him feel ill.

He skipped a few meals because of the persistent queasy feeling he was fighting. The perceptive captain guessed what was going through Joseph's mind and invited him into his office while still a couple of days from Port. "You're thinking about going to find your sister, aren't you? And you're worried you'll run into your father." The captain cut right to the heart of the issue.

"Is it that obvious?" replied Joseph, surprised at how accurate the captain's observations were.

"It is to me, especially after the talk we had while in Hong Kong. Of course, I know about your father and how you feel about him. But I didn't know about your sister. You were her caregiver, her protector for the first years of her life. How could you not be concerned and want to know how she is?"

"Ever since we talked about it while in Hong Kong, it's been gnawing at me. I've almost been obsessed with the thought of finding her. Do you think it strange?" asked Joseph.

"I would think it strange if you weren't obsessed with the idea." The captain continued, "As for your father, consider this. You've been gone from Bristol close to fifteen years. He was drinking heavily when you left. He is probably still drinking heavily or worse. The only time I have seen someone stop drinking heavily is if they get put in jail for some reason, usually drinking related, such as stealing to buy more drink or fighting because of their drinking. There is one more possibility." The captain paused enough to be sure Joseph was listening carefully. "He could be dead."

Joseph stiffened, standing straight at this thought. "I'd never considered that," he said slowly, allowing this new thought to seep into his mind.

The captain continued. His voice was both that of a concerned parent and instructive as a captain to a sailor. "Here are the possibilities as I see them. Your father is either dead, or in jail, or so drink addled he doesn't care if you're around, or—and this is the least likely possibility—he is in a similar condition as when you ran away. If that is the case, you're now as big as he is and much stronger and quicker. In fact, if I were a betting man, and this was a fight in a ring, I'd quickly put down a hundred pounds you would be done with him in less than a minute." This brought a smile to both their faces. The captain could see the tension that had been building in Joseph for weeks leave his body and evaporate. From that night on, Joseph was excited to search for Jemima.

CHAPTER 10

Once the ship was secure at the dock, critical cargo unloaded, and the crew released for some shore time, Joseph was the first one off, just the opposite from most dockings. Even though it had been many years since he'd been to where he grew up, he had no trouble finding the house he was looking for. Some buildings had been added, and even a few streets were new. He purposely walked an extra mile around so he could approach the neighbor's house from the opposite direction and not walk past his old house.

As he turned the last corner, the neighbor's house came into view. He stopped briefly, as emotions were flying through him. The trees were larger, and a few flowers were growing where he remembered weeds and brush before. "Remember," he said to himself as he tried to keep his plan on track, "after this many years, she likely won't be there, but they might know where she is." He realized the chances of finding Jemima anywhere were slim. He felt some of his excitement evaporate as the realities of the situation sank in. Just then, someone who had been out tending the flowers stood up. It was a woman. He shielded his eyes to get a better look at her face. At first he didn't recognize the lady. Then as he shuffled images of women from previous years through his mind, then mentally added fifteen years to what she might look like, a light came on. Maybe it was the woman of the house. He was only seven when he last saw her. He, like most children of that age, filed most females who were not his family in the "other" category—neighbors, store clerks, schoolteachers. This woman had gray hair and a wrinkled, tired look. But there was a resemblance, a familiarity to her. Joseph braced himself as he approached her.

"Excuse me, ma'am," Joseph said. The woman nearly jumped out of her skin as she was concentrating on the blooming flowers she was gathering.

"You scared the breath out of me," she said as she picked up the cutting knife she dropped. "I didn't see you coming."

"I'm sorry. I didn't mean to startle you. I'm Joseph Godfrey and—"

"Joseph Godfrey!" The women cut him off as she eyed him over closely, doing her own mental comparison of images stuffed away in her memory. "I'd given up ever seeing you again." Joseph decided it might be best just to try to look pleasant and be quiet after nearly scaring her to death and revealing his identity. "Yes, I can see it now. You are Joseph. Wow, you've grown a bit. You've grown up, and I've grown old. I suppose you've got a few questions for me? And I have a few questions for you. Let's sit on the porch out of the sun." They made their way a few yards to the porch that had several comfortable chairs and good shade but was open to allow the breeze through.

Their bottoms had barely touched the chairs when her need for information trumped his need for information. "Where have you been, Joseph?" she asked.

"I work on a whaling ship. I've been on that ship since I ran away," Joseph started. "I've been all over the world. It's a good ship, with a good captain that I've grown quite close too. He raised me really since I left here. It's been good for me."

"How did you end up on a whaling ship?" she asked. Joseph paused, realizing the telling of that chain of events could take quite a long time, without getting to the reason for his coming. She realized the reason for the pause and then added, "You can tell me later. I suppose you want to know about Jemima … and your father." All Joseph had to do was look at her and nod. "I'll tell you what I know as soon as I get us each a cup of water. I've been working in those flowers a couple of hours now." She disappeared into the house, and Joseph could hear the noise of her getting the cups, pouring the water, and walking back to the front porch.

"The morning Jemima showed up at our door, hungry, scared, and not sure what was happening, I admit I wasn't surprised. For the next full day, she kept repeating, 'We can no longer stay in our home. Father beats us. Joseph is running away.' That's all she would say. We tried to find you but had no luck. It wasn't long until your father came to our door assuming Jemima might be here and demanded we give her back. My husband got involved. We knew we couldn't keep her here just on what she was saying. My husband finally agreed to turn her over to the sheriff and let him look at things, let him decide what to do. Poor Jemima. The sheriff did agree to let her stay here for a couple of days while he checked into it and waited to see if you would turn up. She ate like it was the last food on earth during those days. After a few days when you didn't turn up, word filtered back that there had been an incident down at the docks. We thought maybe you did get away on a ship. By that time, your father had settled down some and realized that, without you at home, he couldn't keep Jemima. So he told the sheriff he would send her to your mother." The wild-eyed, contorted look on Joseph's face said it all. The women's hand flew to her mouth, and she gasped, "You didn't know she was still alive." After a few seconds pause, she continued, "Your father told us, quite bluntly, to never, never say anything to you kids about her leaving." Another a long pause, she said, "He told you she was dead, didn't he?" Tears came to Joseph's eyes as he nodded.

"Do you know where she, or they, are?" he quickly asked.

Her silence was deafening. She finally said, "After about a week, your father and the sheriff came and got her and just said she was going to your mother's. We asked where that was, but the sheriff said it was best not to say."

Joseph was deflated, realizing that finding them after this long was unlikely. A few more seconds went by, and then Joseph asked the question he had been dreading but knew he had to ask if he was to find any level of resolution. "What about my father? What do you know about him?"

"After the incident with Jemima, we rarely spoke to him or even saw him. The last time I remember was a few years ago. My husband and I went to the tool and rope store down by the docks. We saw him sitting up against the building—at least we thought it was him. He was not in good condition, drunk, ragged clothes. After we had bought what we came for, my husband asked the clerk if that was William Godfrey. I'm sorry, Joseph, this may be hard to hear, but I'll tell you as near as I can remember word for word. The clerk said, 'Yeah, that's him, or what's left of him. He drank so much he couldn't work and spends his days, most of them, in front of my store, begging for enough coins to buy one more drink. But winter's coming ... I don't expect he'll be in front of my store next spring.'" The woman was quiet, realizing she had dumped a huge load on Joseph, allowing him time to process the information.

Joseph finished his cup of water, handed the cup to the woman, and avoided looking at her so she couldn't see the tears that filled his eyes. He graciously thanked her and stood up to leave. The woman's heart was breaking as she saw this strong young man who had bravely walked up onto her porch leave with slumped shoulders, head down, shuffling along her pathway as he left. Joseph got near the street when he stopped, straightened a little, turned to the woman, and said, "Thanks again for telling me about my family. I realize I haven't told you about working on the whaling ship. Maybe next time. I'm doing good. Life is good for me."

CHAPTER 11

It was summer, and the ship was headed north in the Atlantic as it often did at this time of year. Each day was noticeably longer the farther north they traveled. It didn't get dark enough for normal sleep till long after midnight. This trip took them close to Iceland. Joseph had never been to Iceland. It didn't sound like a very inviting place, Iceland. When Joseph learned the captain intended to stop a few days to resupply some food items, canvas, and rope, he envisioned a dark, cold, uninviting, and inhospitable place. What he would experience was very pleasant and educational. Among other things, Joseph learned the country is one of the most active in the world for volcanoes. A few years before, a volcano erupted underneath a glacier, raining down fire and ice together. The result was a flood of both water and lava, a rare sight.

While traveling in the North Atlantic off the coast of Canada, Captain Fitzgerald was at the wheel in midafternoon and instructing some of the crew as they cleaned and repainted the hulls of their harpoon boats. He stopped talking in midsentence. The crew stopped and stood, waiting for him to finish his instructions. After a long minute of silence, the men looked closer and were alarmed to see him slumped over the wheel, finally collapsing to the deck. A shout went out to the first mate, and the men rushed over to see what the matter was. His eyes were locked open in a distant stare, and when they spoke to him, he looked as if he was acknowledging their question but didn't respond. The first mate arrived and took the wheel, then instructed the men to carry him below to his bunk. The ship's doctor was summoned. He wasn't really a doctor but had proven the best at stitching up the men when needed and administering various elixirs and ointments.

"Doc" looked him over carefully, poking in various places and quietly muttering while nodding or shaking his head in an attempt to look professional. Then he announced the captain was just overworked and needed some rest. He would be fine in the morning. A couple of hours later, Joseph went to the captain's bunk to look in on him. When he spoke his name, the captain slowly opened his eyes and groaned. Joseph was shocked at what he saw. The captain's eyes were bloodshot and sunk deep in their sockets. His lips were a light blue. When he touched his hand, it was ice cold and very clammy. He was barely breathing. Joseph quivered and stumbled back a step when the words came blasting into his mind, *He's going to die!* Joseph wasn't prepared for this. He could hardly breathe himself.

As he left the cabin, a couple of sailors asked, "How is he?" Joseph couldn't answer and simply look down and shook his head. In a few minutes, the whole ship knew things looked bad for the captain. An hour later, Doc went in to examine his progress and found him dead. He stumbled out on deck, sobbing out the words, "He's dead."

Two hours later, the crew gathered on deck for a farewell ceremony and to commit him to the sea. The first mate said a few nonreligious but laudatory words and then gave the nod for Captain Fitzgerald to be committed to the sea. The sound of the splash was a delineation mark in each man's heart, before the captain, and after the captain. The men stood, frozen as the reality of their new situation slowly seeped into their minds and souls. *We have no captain*, seemed to scream in their minds while the silence smothered them. After nearly thirty minutes, the first mate stepped forward and announced some reassignments of duties and work shifts. To this someone in the crew yelled, "We want Joseph to be captain!" followed by "Aye, aye" and a few others clapping.

"So you want Joseph, do you?" said the first mate. "That's not the tradition of the sea. What about tradition?"

Someone responded, "Joseph has been on the ship the longest," which was true. Joseph had been on the ship for over twenty years. The first mate had been brought on the ship about seven years ago when the ship he was on was decommissioned. He had been on the sea about twenty years before that. When the first mate joined them, Joseph was still a teenager, but everyone knew the captain was grooming him to be the first mate at the right opportunity.

There was no question the first mate had his supporters. But if there were a democratic election, Joseph would easily win. However, ships at sea are not democratic. And they don't have elections. It's more military, even on a civilian ship. The first mate stared at Joseph as if he was being challenged to a duel or a fight. Joseph hadn't said a word. This was a turning point, a fork in the road that could forever change the direction they were traveling. "Joseph, Joseph, Joseph," part of the crew softly chanted. If they had they not just buried the captain, the chanting would have been much louder and demanding. Joseph's eyes met the stare of the first mate. Both of them knew the position of captain was Joseph's if he wanted. The other man was older, but physically they were about the same size and strength. Joseph had exhibited more talent and leadership. Plus, he had the support of a majority of the men.

Captain Fitzgerald had taught Joseph many lessons, among them being, "Don't ever detract from a man making a good decision, be honest, and don't trifle with tradition."

With these lessons playing out in his mind, Joseph spoke up, nodding to the first mate, "You can be captain." Immediately Joseph felt relief that the issue had been defused. It was followed by the gratifying thought, *Who really has the most power, the captain or the one who makes him captain?* His next thought was even more dramatic; he would leave the ship at the next opportunity.

As Joseph awoke the next morning, it took a few minutes to realize what had happened the previous day was reality and not just a bad dream. The captain's death had been sudden and unexpected. He reflected on his decision not to become the captain and reviewed again his decision to leave the ship. He still felt the same. He didn't know where it might lead him, but he felt the time had come for him to leave the ship. He had mentioned his decision to leave to no one and thought it best not to say anything about it. Because of the captain's death, the ship redirected its course toward New York City. This was not the closest port, but news of what had transpired needed to be sent back to the ship's owners in England, and New York was the nearest port with regular travel to England to take the news.

It took another six days to reach New York. Arriving at sunset, the ship anchored about a half mile off shore and was waiting until morning to dock. As Joseph contemplated leaving the ship, pangs of fear began welling up inside. His first thought was to simply find another ship to work on. But what if he couldn't find another crew he could work with? If he worked on the land, what was he qualified to do? These thoughts pushed him to tell his friend George what he was planning. George had been a good friend to Joseph for several years now. He was younger than Joseph but was very encouraging and offered to go with Joseph, which was good. With George going, Joseph was confident they would be all right. George Coleman had joined the ship a few years earlier, and they were from the same area in England, had the same way of speaking, and shared many views. They were fast friends and had similar thoughts about life.

To avoid confrontation, early the next morning, George and Joseph took a small chest containing all they had accumulated over the past two decades and launched a small rowboat to take them to shore. They were as quiet as they could be but still caused enough noise to alert a few sailors, who notified the new captain they were leaving. The new captain and a few of his buddies gathered at the rail and began to jeer at them. George and Joseph thought it best not to respond and concentrated on casting off the ropes and rowing away. They had only moved a few feet from the ship when a sailor on board threw a harpoon at the small boat. George and Joseph jumped out of the way, narrowly avoiding being struck. The boat was not so lucky. The harpoon crashed through the bottom of the boat, breaking a twelve-inch hole in the bottom. Water gushed in, and all efforts to plug the hole failed. In seconds, the boat capsized and headed for the bottom of the harbor. Joseph dove down and was able to grab hold of the chest and frantically tried to get back to the surface. A few seconds later, he realized he had to abandon his effort with the heavy chest to save himself. He broke the surface of the water, gasping great gulps of air. He looked up at the ship for his crewmates, but they had scampered away from the railing after the harpoon crashed through the rowboat. George, with his clothes soaked and heavy, could barely keep his head above water. Joseph realized their only hope of survival was to strip off any extra clothes and try to swim to shore. They picked what they thought was the closest point on shore and would swim a hundred yards and then float on their backs a few minutes to catch their breath and regain some energy. Then they'd repeat the process. Two hours later, the two men barely pulled themselves out of the water onto the shore, their feet still getting wet as the waves came in.

CHAPTER 12

After most of an hour, Joseph sat up and noticed the only clothing either of them had on was a thin pair of underwear. He wondered out loud, "What do we do now? We have no money, no clothes, and nothing to trade or barter with." They had set foot on this new land with absolutely nothing, totally destitute. For over twenty-five years, Joseph felt safe on the ship and was provided all he needed. In two hours, he went from having all he needed to having nothing and no Captain Fitzgerald to provide. It was completely up to him. He thought of a similar situation over twenty-five years earlier when he struck out on his own, trusting his desire to survive and praying for some heavenly help in finding the next stepping stone. That's what he must do again.

He said a silent prayer and then said to George, eyeing a livery stable down the street, "We'll have to start at the bottom. We'll do whatever we need to get a meal and some clothes. There is most likely a man running that stable down the street. He may laugh at our underwear, but maybe he'll help us out. We'll offer to shovel manure, you know, clean his stable." To be the least conspicuous, the two stayed off the road and walked behind some buildings to the stable. Approaching the stable from the alley behind, they saw a man pitching hay to some horses. He didn't notice them walking up until they spoke.   "Can you help us out, Mr.? We're willing to work," Joseph said. He thought he'd better include the work offer in the same breath unless the man thought they were just beggars looking for a handout.   The man eyed them over carefully, chuckled a little, and then said, "I've heard of men losing their horse in a poker game, but I've never seen someone who lost their pants."

Joseph and George stared at the ground and nodded slightly. That was as good a story as any at this point, and they decided to let it slide for now. The man scratched his chin and muttered, "Cleaning the stalls in your underwear will never do." Then it was like a light turned on inside his head. He continued, "Several months ago, a man left his horse and a trunk and said he'd be back to settle up with me in a few days. He never returned. That trunk is up in the loft. You could probably find something in there that would cover your backside and some shoes that might fit. If, by the end of the day you've done a decent job, you can keep the clothes, and my wife will fix you dinner. By the way, my name is Hank. What do they call you?"

"My name is Joseph, and this is George," he said as he extended his hand. Hank was hesitant to shake somebody's hand with no clothes on. After looking around to be sure no one was watching, he quickly shook his hand.

No money was going to change hands, but the two most important items for the day could be achieved, food and clothing.

"After you get some clothes on, there are four stalls here and four stalls on the other side that need attention," he said as he waved his hands over his head more in an effort to impress upon the men he meant business than actually to show direction. "The pitchforks and wheelbarrow are over there against that wall. You can dump your loads out back on the pile that's already started." Then he disappeared to the front of the stable where a customer was waiting to talk to him.

There were several changes of clothes in the trunk. The man who left it must have been a bit portly. The clothes were too big for the lean and hardened bodies of Joseph and George. But they had no alternative. They were grateful to have anything to dress in. Joseph and George were no strangers to hard work. But this kind of work was new to them. They had never seen a pitchfork before, let alone seen how to use it. They did the best they could, and after about thirty minutes, Hank came by to check on them. He was impressed the men were working hard, each in a different stall. They were even starting to show some sweat. But he was very unimpressed at how much work they were getting done. It didn't take long to see the problem.

"Have you never seen a pitchfork before? Here, let me show you how to use one." Hank took Joseph's pitchfork and with a couple of scoops in less than five seconds had forked up more manure than the two men had in thirty minutes. The light went on in George and Joseph's minds, and they tackled the stalls, deep with manure, with new efficiency and energy.

Hank checked on their progress again in the early afternoon and was impressed enough to say, "If you men keep it up, I'll have to feed you supper tonight." Then he flagged down a boy who was passing by and sent a message home to his wife that they'd probably have two extra men for supper tonight. This wasn't unusual for Hank. He often hired some day labor to help at the stable, but usually it was for the going rate, one dollar a day, with no food included.

They were just finishing up about four o clock when Hank came by once more to check on the stalls. "These stalls haven't been this clean since they were new. I'd even sleep in one if I had to. I'll be heading home soon. It's a bit early, but you'll need a little extra time to wash up." That's just what Joseph was thinking. He felt dirty, sweaty, and smelly and was not anxious to be at the same table with a woman without cleaning up.

"I don't ever remember ever having dinner with a woman at the table," Joseph remarked to George after Hank had walked away. During the twenty-five years at sea, dinner had always been with the other sailors. On those occasions when Joseph ate a meal on shore, it was always alone or with the captain or one of the other sailors. This, indeed, was proving to be a remarkable departure from his familiar life on the sea. Joseph was feeling queasy and a bit fearful. He told himself if he found this type of work too strange, he could always hire on with another ship. But that thought didn't sit well with him. A new ship with a new crew could be disastrous. Joseph realized his time on the ship was not normal. Being only a young boy to begin with, the captain and crew were especially careful to shield him from the riggers, the language, and many of the harsh sights and circumstances most sailors experienced. The captain reinforced this standard by sharply correcting and criticizing those sailors who violated that standard.

Hank's wife was making mutton stew when the message from Hank arrived. "Good thing he let me know early," she said to the messenger. Then she handed him a cookie for his service. She peeled a few more potatoes, scrubbed a couple more carrots, and added two more cups of water to the pot containing the small amount of mutton that was to be their meat for the day. It was always a roll of the dice when Hank brought workers home. Some were gentlemen and were interesting to talk with. Others were rough, crass, rude, and seemed to delight in how vulgar they could be. If that was the case, Hank's wife usually found a reason to busy herself in the kitchen. Hank tolerated it, but as soon as the last spoonful left the plate, Hank was opening the door, inviting them to leave.

That night, Hank and his wife were mesmerized by the two men at their table. It wasn't unusual to rub shoulders with sailors in this seaport town, but these two proved to be courteous, pleasant, and quite articulate when telling of their whaling adventures in various parts of the world. By late that evening, all were feeling good about the day's accomplishments and their new friends. "Where are you going to sleep tonight?" asked Hank.

Joseph and George gave a blank stare at each other, shook their heads, and said, "We don't know." They quickly added, "But we'll find a place."

"I know where there are eight stalls clean enough to sleep in. Just put down some extra, fresh straw and you'll have as good a bed as anywhere in town. And in the morning, I'll mention to a couple of other stables in the area that you need work."

Shoveling manure was not the kind of work they wanted, but it might get them a little money in their pockets. They took Hank up on his offer to sleep at his stable, thanked his wife for the tasty meal, and said their good-byes.

Laying on the fresh straw, Joseph immediately missed the rocking of the ship and the sounds he'd grown accustomed to. He realized he was looking at a new and very different part of his life. He had little memory of his life before his life on the sea. Questions started popping into his mind. *How do I, or rather we, make a living? What kind of work should we pursue? What kinds of work are available? Will I have to learn how to handle cattle or horses? How do I stay warm in the winter?* On the ship, they had always sailed where the weather was warm. *What's it like to be in a snowstorm?* And there were dozens more questions.

As Joseph squirmed a little in the straw to make it as comfortable as possible, he commented to George, "Our first working day on land was not too bad, George. It will be interesting to see what tomorrow brings."

CHAPTER 13

The next thing he knew, it was getting light outside, and he heard the noise of someone entering the stable. Any alarm he felt was soon dismissed by Hank saying, "I thought you may still be sleeping after that tough day yesterday. Here, I brought you a couple of biscuits left over from last night." Hank tossed each of them a couple of biscuits.

Joseph and George thanked Hank for the biscuits, the meal the previous night, and the work and then excused themselves to see where else they might find work. It wasn't long before word got around that they were good workers. They were often committed for several days out. After several weeks, they wanted something more permanent and ventured outside of the city to look for farm work.

Joseph realized that hoeing corn was boring, mind-numbing work. It was hot. It was tedious. But it needed to be done, and Mr. Reeves was willing to take a chance on these two sailors who showed up at his door asking for work. "What does a sailor know about hoeing corn or hoeing anything, or growing anything for that matter?" Mr. Reeves asked. "But it's not that hard. I can show you what you need to know in thirty seconds." He showed them what a corn plant looked like. "Anything else, everything else is considered a weed and should be hoed up."

Growing corn in New Jersey was marginal at best. The growing season was usually too short for corn, which did much better several hundred miles south. Oats, wheat, and barley did much better there, but Mr. Reeves was growing five acres as an experiment to see if he could get a crop.

They worked hard until midafternoon and then stopped for a short rest. "I sure could use a bucket of ocean about now," Joseph said to George.

"It looks like you've got an ocean dripping off your face," replied George. The jug of water they brought with them that morning was about gone, and what was left was so hot it almost burned the tongue. It was a tough decision whether to continue being thirsty with a mouth so dry they could spit cotton or have a sip of water so hot it scalded the lips. About then, Joseph saw one of the most beautiful sights he had ever seen—someone, in fact two people, bringing a pitcher of something out toward the field where they were working. He immediately assumed that what was in the pitcher was liquid and cold, or at least cool. And the fact that it was two females was not lost on him either. As the women drew closer, Joseph's eyes left what was being carried and migrated to the faces of the ones doing the carrying. Now he was very interested! No, *they* were very interested!

"I don't think I've ever seen a prettier sight than that lady dressed in brown coming this way," Joseph said.

"Unless it's the lady dressed in green walking along with her," replied George. The conversation that followed when the two groups met would have fit in a thimble, but what was communicated with wide eyes, big grins, and feet shuffling in the dirt would fill volumes.

"Pa said to come bring you two a drink," said Ann Eliza, the older of the two, in her early twenties, and the oldest of the Reeves family of nine. Her sister Mary was three years younger. That was the only complete sentence uttered at this first meeting. The water, cool from a forty-foot well, pulled just a few minutes before, was consumed in great gulps in the dusty, dry mouths of the two men. At the conclusion of the gulping, both men, their tongues inoperable, just nodded their gratitude with nods so exaggerated most people would consider them a bow. The women, trying to contain their giddiness, curtsied, spun on their heels, and scampered as quickly as possible out of earshot. For the rest of the day, both men felt no heat, felt no pain, and were not thirsty in the least. They were lost in the thoughts of what had just happened and energized by the hope that maybe it might happen again tomorrow.

It did happen again the next day. In fact, it became a regular occurrence, and they started spending evenings together as well. Over two decades of sailing and whaling experiences from all over the world filled many hours of talk, not only for the two women, but often the whole family would listen for hours. And to reciprocate, the Reeves family was pleased to elaborate what life was like in the fairly new nation of the United States. Mr. Reeves had been born shortly after the Revolutionary War. To clear ground for farming, build a cabin, corrals, and a root cellar was a different way of living for Joseph and George. Life was sustained by planting crops and hunting. This stretched their understanding of what it took to survive on land as opposed to living from the sea. Joseph could sail a ship, but driving a wagon and handling horses or oxen took a lot of practice and resulted in more than a few mishaps. They now had to learn how to judge the temperament of a horse and anticipate what it might do in different circumstances like rain or muddy roads or at night versus the day. How to handle them in different conditions was challenging for the men. Mr. Reeves was a bit surprised to find these men were honest, hardworking, even spiritual men, unlike most of the sailors Mr. Reeves had known previously.

It wasn't too many months before the "marriage" word started creeping into the minds and conversations of the two couples, Joseph and Ann Eliza, George and Mary. Until a few months ago, Joseph had always supposed he'd never marry, as was the case with the captain and most other sailors. But he also assumed he'd always be a sailor on a whaling ship. This paradigm shift came one afternoon as he and Ann Eliza were hauling milk and eggs to town to trade for heavy fabric for Mrs. Reeves to sew winter clothes for the family. Here he was, Ann Eliza by his side, bumping down the road on a beautiful, clear autumn afternoon. "After I ran away from home and got used to life as a whaler, I felt like I had arrived at what I'd do the rest of my life. I enjoyed that life and seeing different parts of the world. Then the captain died, and in a few hours everything changed."

"How do you feel about your life now?" Ann Eliza asked in an effort to keep him talking.

"The difference in my life between the whaling ship and where I am now and where I'm headed is striking. I'm happier than I ever hoped I could be. The only thing that would make it better is to have someone special to share it with. Ann Eliza, will you marry me?" Ann Eliza was thrilled with the proposal. It was that afternoon they set the date to get married and started talking about their life together.

It was no surprise that George and Mary were having similar conversations about marriage. However, the timing and the place they were married was influenced by the vast personality difference between Ann Eliza and Mary. Mary was determined to show her individuality by not following in the exact footsteps of her sister. Several months after the marriage of Joseph and Ann Eliza, George and Mary eloped to Niagra Falls, New York, to be married. But both couples started their married lives by settling on the Reeves farm with the men working for Mr. Reeves.

CHAPTER 14

Joseph arose before dawn. It would be a good hour before the sun peeked over the horizon, but there were chores to be done. He fed and watered the horses, and after the animals had their fill, they were fitted with harnesses and hooked up to the wagon that had been loaded the night before with sacks of oats and barley. Joseph and George were to take the load the twenty miles into town, sell or trade the grain, gather up a list of foodstuff and supplies to last them the winter, and then return to the farm. It would be a long day if everything went reasonably well. There was frost on the wagon seat and a thin layer of ice on the watering trough. George broke the ice and scooped out the chunks of ice so the horses could get a good drink after eating the hay Joseph had fed them.

Before the horses were done eating, the men went back in the house to have their breakfast and then started out. Each couple had their own bedroom with a common kitchen between them. The wives had fixed them oatmeal, bacon, and eggs and had prepared some sandwiches for the men to take for later on. They stopped briefly as they drove away to get some last-minute instructions from Mr. Reeves. Not much was said for the first several miles as the men continued to wake up. As they became more alert, it was easy to admire the turning leaves and the frosty air.

At late morning, still a few miles from town, the men came upon a man walking in the same direction. "Are you headed to town?" asked Joseph as they came along side.

"Yes, I am," replied the man. "I've been walking since sunup. It shouldn't be too much farther, should it?"

"It's still three to four miles," said Joseph. "Get on, and we'll give you a ride." George moved to a sack behind the driver's seat, allowing the man to sit next to Joseph. He was carrying several books in a sack. "I'm Joseph, and this is George. We've come about fifteen miles this morning, headed to town to do some trading and to stock up for the winter. You?"

"I'm Brother Jacobs. I mean Henry Jacobs," the man said.

"Brother Jacobs?" questioned Joseph. "Are you a preacher?"

The man explained he was an elder in the Church of Jesus Christ of Latter-day Saints, also called the Mormons. He was on a mission to contact as many as he could in that area and explain their beliefs.

"Well, at least for the next few miles, you've got a captive audience. Tell us what you believe," said Joseph.

Brother Jacobs started to explain about the Book of Mormon, Joseph Smith, and the organization of the church. Questions came flooding to the minds of George and Joseph, and they peppered the man with the questions. In no time, they were in town, and they pulled up in front of the store. The conversation was so lively no one got off the wagon for a full forty-five minutes after they arrived. Finally, a young man came out of the store and asked if they needed help unloading the wagon. This snapped the men to the realization they still had a job to do, and they needed to move along if they were to start back before the day grew too late.

"Our business here will take a couple of hours," Joseph said to Brother Jacobs as he started to leave. "We'd like to invite you to ride back with us. We'll put you up for the night, and you'll have a chance to discuss this with our wives." Brother Jacobs agreed, and he went off to talk to some others, but not before he left a copy of the Book of Mormon with George and Joseph from his sack. Joseph put it under the seat of the wagon as he went to discuss the details of the trade with the storeowner. Joseph found himself distracted as his mind kept circling back to some of the things he had heard. Had he focused on the business of the day, he certainly could have gotten a better deal, but he was glad to get the trading over with so he could mindlessly begin unloading the sacks of grain and mull over what he had just heard from Brother Jacobs. Joseph had traveled the world for over twenty years, and never had he heard anything that intrigued him like this did. George was having similar thoughts as the two unloaded the wagon. They were blindly doing the job before them as they thought about what Brother Jacobs had said. Joseph was anxious to get the supplies collected and get back on the road so they could continue their discussion.

The two men sat in the wagon loaded with the acquired supplies, waiting for Brother Jacobs to return. The sun continued its journey to the western horizon. Joseph became more and more depressed with each passing minute, finally shaking his head in discouragement. "What are you thinking?" asked George.

"It doesn't look like he's going to show up," replied Joseph, a bit disgusted Brother Jacobs hadn't shown up. "We can't wait any longer. It will already be past dark when we get back." Joseph slapped the reins against the backs of the impatient horses. Just as they jerked to a start, Brother Jacobs appeared from around the corner, out of breath and a bit frazzled.

"I'm here! I'm here!" he shouted. "I'm sorry I'm late. I just couldn't get away from the mayor. I finally had just to cut him off and walk out. I need to catch my breath," he said as he settled into the seat next to Joseph.

They were at least a mile out of town before anyone spoke. Brother Jacobs pulled out a big chunk of deer jerky and offered some to the two men. The sandwiches sent by their wives were long gone, and the jerky was welcome and tasty. George asked the first question, which opened the floodgates to a myriad of other questions. The discussion was nonstop until they pulled up in front of the bunkhouse. Mr. Reeves appeared from the main house, and introductions were made all around. Mr. Reeves volunteered to feed and put the horses away for the night as the others dragged themselves into the bunkhouse to meet Ann Eliza and Mary. Mr. Reeves noticed it was after midnight before the lights were turned down in the bunkhouse.

The next morning, the conversation was brisk. After breakfast, Brother Jacobs thanked them for their hospitality and said he was going to the next county for about a week, and if it was all right, he would return and would like to stay another night. As Brother Jacobs left the farm, Joseph turned to the others and quietly said, "We have a lot to think about the next few days." He picked up his hat and went out to the barn to check on the stock.

Not much was said about the encounter over the next few days, but there was no question each of the two couples was in deep thought about what had been presented. Brother Jacobs's parting words were, "Think about what we've been discussing. Pray about it. And if it feels right, I challenge you to be baptized when I return." Several nights later after supper, the small talk about what happened that day on the farm trailed off. After a full five minutes of silence, Joseph straightened himself, cleared his throat, looked directly at Ann Eliza and then at George, and said strongly, "It does feel right!"

Ann Eliza looked directly back at him answered, "Yes, it does feel right."

George and Mary said, almost in unison, nodding their heads, "I agree." When Brother Jacobs returned, the two couples were baptized in the creek about a half mile from the house. Mr. and Mrs. Reeves asked a lot of questions and showed a lot of interest but were not ready to follow suit.

CHAPTER 15

After they joined the Mormon Church, their lives began changing dramatically, some in a good way, some not so good. The rest of the Reeves family showed significant interest and asked a lot of questions, especially Matilda, a sister to Ann Eliza and Mary in her midteens.

"I have a hard time believing or even understanding what our preacher is telling us about God and heaven," commented Matilda one evening as most of the family had gathered after supper under the shade of some cottonwood trees. She continued, "How can I relate to or pray to something I can't understand?"

"What I can't believe is God the Father and Christ appearing to a fourteen-year-old boy," Mr. Reeves injected. "I'd like to believe it. It makes more sense than what I've been taught all my life. But, to me, it's just too fantastic."

"Too good to be true," replied Joseph. "That's exactly what I first thought as well. But I couldn't get it out of my mind. It was irritating me. So I decided I had to pray about it, like Elder Jacobs said, to either get it out of my mind or find out if it is true. It didn't take long. I don't know how to describe it. It was an overwhelming peace, like nothing else mattered at that moment—the crops, the animals, the weather, you know, most of the things we worry about every day." Matilda was hanging on Joseph's every word. The rest of the Reeves were interested and respectful but more distant.

When in town, people started avoiding them on the street, and storekeepers, normally eager to chat and exchange various news items from around the area, became brief in their conversation. When transaction were completed, they quickly moved to begin helping others in the store. As long as they were on the farm, they were excited about what they had learned and enjoyed discussing it amongst themselves. But when they had occasion to go to town, they felt very uncomfortable and kept the trip as short as possible.

As they attended church, they found most others had similar experiences. But the sermons were always uplifting and enlightening. Joseph was finding that many of the things he had often thought and felt in his heart were being taught at church. He found himself in deep thought, oblivious to others and events around him, comparing his life experiences to the teachings of the church. He found himself hungering for more and more information. Joseph and George spent most of every day at work discussing what had been the latest doctrine taught and how it was a good fit with what they already believed.

One day while the men were raking newly cut hay into piles, Joseph thought again of when he ran away from home and hid on the whaling ship—being such a young boy with the courage and foresight to accomplish such a feat, to even know which way to go to the docks, to locate the only ship with a compassionate, understanding, and exemplary captain, a ship that would be leaving the very next day. He recalled what he had said to plead his case so that the sailor who discovered him and the captain wouldn't put him off the ship. And then he started a life of learning about the sea and the cultures and climates of the world. He kept turning this over and over in his mind. He stopped raking and leaned on his rake, all the time nodding and shaking his head as the events played out in his mind. George continued to make progress down his row toward the end of the field. When he got to the end, he looked around and was puzzled to see Joseph at the other end of the field being quite animated, as if he was talking to an invisible person. George hollered at him a couple of times, with no response. Then George began working his way back on the next row over, all the time watching Joseph out of the corner of his eye. When George got near the other end of the field, there was no change in Joseph. He was still leaning on his rake, nodding and shaking his head with an occasional hand gesture.

"Joseph!" George yelled, "What are you doing?" This finally brought Joseph back into the present.

Joseph shook his head like he was trying to shake off a stubborn fog and get some clarity. Then he said, "I just got to thinking about what I've experienced so far in my life and what I've learned, and I'm amazed. My head is swimming. Did I ever tell you that my dad was a drunk and would beat me several times a week, and …" This story lasted the rest of the day, all the way home, and through supper. The two couples ate supper together and then spent part of the evening in each other's company. Joseph had told Ann Eliza and George bits and pieces of his history, but this time, it was as if everything lined up and spilled out. At last Joseph took a deep breath, looked closely at the others in the room, and announced, "We need to go to Nauvoo, now!"

Nauvoo was the center of the Mormon Church at this time. It was located in Illinois on the banks of the Mississippi River. It was a swampy, mosquito-infested area that few others were interested in. The Mormons had been driven from place to place for years, mostly because of their "peculiar" beliefs. Then, as their numbers grew, other settlers feared they would all vote in a block, upsetting the balance of power. They were also antislavery, which was always a contentious subject. About 1839, they selected Commerce, Illinois, as a gathering place in hopes of being mostly a community to themselves. They renamed it Nauvoo. They went to work draining the swamps and building roads and buildings. It grew to a city of about twelve thousand before the Mormons left. It was larger than Chicago at the time.

The next morning, the two couples started toward Nauvoo, Illinois, about eight hundred miles. They had previously pooled a meager amount of money to buy an old wagon and two, nearly dead horses. To say the horses were long in the tooth would be an understatement, but it was all they could afford. The wagon was bare, as they owned little but the clothes they were wearing. They did have one gun between them to shoot some game, and they fished a little at every stream they passed. Otherwise, they counted on the kindness of those occupying the occasional homestead to share some food with them.

"I can't explain it," Joseph blurted out one morning to the group after traveling several miles with no words spoken. "When George and I were on the ship, we had work, and we had all the food we cared to eat, some of it quite exotic food from all over the world. We had a bunk to sleep in and a trunk full of trinkets and treasures we'd picked up from different countries, and now we have nearly nothing. But I feel more optimistic, more settled, more confident, and richer than ever before. Why? What do you think, George?"

"Well, it could have something to do with these two fine, young ladies in this wagon riding with us," George said as he winked at Mary and pulled her close for a hug. "It could also have something to do with the understanding we have that God loves and values us enough to speak to and direct men on earth today. I feel a sense of relief. Joseph, do you remember times when we were at sea, with no other ships in sight? We saw no other ships or landmarks for weeks at a time. Only the clouds above and the sea below? You get to wondering, at least I did, is this all there is? Is there a God, and is there a plan? And what if this is all there is? It's a scary thought. It's a terrifying thought."

"I have had those thoughts, George," replied Joseph. "But it was always followed with the realization that this is too magnificent and at the same time too delicate not to be under the watch of some grand power. And when I heard the message of Brother Jacobs, it all clicked. This is what I've been looking for."

The trip to Nauvoo took nearly two months. They were unsure as to whether the horses would last until they reached their destination. Finding enough food was another item that was always a concern. When they would find a homestead, Joseph learned it made a big difference as to how he phrased the plea for some assistance. For example, he would say, "We're headed out to the frontier west of Chicago. Could you give us a meal to *help us on our way?*" This implied that if they were to share some of their food with them, they would leave. It usually got them a meal, but there were many other areas where no homesteads were in sight. They made do with a rabbit or squirrel they shot or some berries they happened to find. When it rained, their only cover was under the wagon.

When they finally arrived in Nauvoo, they drove up and down a few streets to become acquainted with the city and then drove by the site where the temple was being constructed. At this point, only the foundation was visible. That still gave a sense of the size and how it would be positioned. A rough charcoal sketch had been nailed to a post so those who passed by could see what the church had in mind. They sat in silence trying to wrap their minds around what was being built and what it meant. Joseph found himself muttering over and over, "A temple, a temple, a temple?" Over the next several years, the temple would become many things, a symbol of sacrifice and faith, a source of spiritual strength and direction, and most of all, a source of enlightenment and understanding.

Joseph felt very comfortable living among church members. The city was flooded with many more just like them, nearly destitute, with few material possessions but with great faith and a desire to work to achieve their goals. At the same time, there were many who lost their faith and left the area or, worse, worked against the church. They were constantly being harassed and troubled by those outside Nauvoo. Their leader and prophet, Joseph Smith, was under constant threat from mobs and civil authorities. Joseph and George even took their turns being bodyguards for the prophet.

They took comfort in being among so many of like mind. There were many meetings. Joseph couldn't believe how many. But he usually felt uplifted and a bit stronger after the meetings. He often asked himself if he regretted the decision to come here. It had not been an easy life. After considering it all, he had few regrets and felt he was where he should be.

The city continued to grow, and the trouble with outsiders escalated. The outsiders felt threatened by such a large group that was organized, industrious, and could influence things politically. But it was more than that. After an incident where some horses were stolen and other livestock turned loose and driven off, two brothers went looking for the horses. They found them several miles away in a coral. No one else was around, so they proceeded to take the horses back. The thieves returned just then and hung one of the brothers there on the spot. The other brother was told to go back and tell the others they'd better get out of Illinois if they didn't want to see more people hung.

Joseph said to George, "Outsiders ridicule our beliefs, but why should they care? Many other Christian churches have beliefs considered different, but there aren't the threats and physical violence directed toward them. Why us?"

"I've asked myself the same question," replied George. "What we believe must upset Satan for people to act like they do."

CHAPTER 16

Joseph could point to specific events in his life that were fixed in his mind to stand as points of demarcation, the before and after—when he vowed never to be beaten again by his father, the day the captain gathered Joseph in his arms and comforted him when he spilled ink on the sea maps, the day he and George left the ship and swam to shore, the day Ann Eliza and Mary Reeves brought water to Joseph and George while they worked in their father's field, the day Brother Jacobs told them about the Mormon Church, and June 27, 1844. This would be the day to set in motion a different direction for George, Joseph, and their wives—in fact, most all the Mormons. It was the day Joseph Smith and his brother Hyrum were assassinated while being held in Carthage jail for their own "protection."

The enemies of the church were sure this would promptly break up the group. And, in fact, it did precipitate the organization of several splinter groups, mostly revolving around who should serve as successor and how such a successor should be put in place. However, the non-Mormons were disappointed to see that their efforts did not disband the group, and they continued their harassment to drive them from the state.

In February 1845, the weather was cold enough to freeze the Mississippi River. And it was the beginning of an exodus of first a few hundred and then thousands of Mormons who left Illinois and headed west. The night before the two couples left, they worshiped in the barely completed temple that they had admired the first day they came into town.

The next night, the group left their home in Nauvoo and headed west across the Mississippi River. It was bitter cold. That was both a blessing and a curse. They were dressed poorly, and from the start, it was a struggle to keep fingers and toes from freezing. And now there were children. George and Mary had a young boy, two years old. Joseph and Ann Eliza had a four-year-old, a two-year-old, and a one-year-old, all boys, and Ann Eliza was expecting again but was not far enough along to hamper their progress. The cold weather had frozen the river. So instead of lining up for their turn to ride a ferry across, they simply walked across. However, walking was risky. Not only was it slick, but ice chunks floating down the river had frozen in place, making the surface very uneven. The children had to be carried the whole time. Being so poor, they had little else to carry. They still had one gun between them and one knife. The hope was that when they got to the other side, they could fashion some type of shelter to block the wind enough to build a fire and gather some warmth.

They walked mostly in silence as the gravity of their situation settled over them. This was a life-or-death situation, especially for the children. Suddenly Joseph began to chuckle and then chuckle some more.

"What could you possibly find to laugh about on a night like this?" George asked.

"I was just thinking," Joseph replied, "how similar this situation is to Moses parting the Red Sea and leading the Israelites away from Pharaoh's army. You can't deny that was a miracle. This is also a miracle. The Red Sea got the Israelites away from their enemies, just like the Mississippi is getting us away from our enemies. This river rarely freezes, and for it to freeze tonight, of all nights, is a miracle, like the parting of the Red Sea." Joseph was not chuckling because he thought the similarities were humorous but because he saw the similarities as a coincidence he found remarkable.

The conversation was a welcome distraction from the serious matters they were all focused on. George continued, "Joseph, what do you think is more risky, heading out in the middle of winter to parts unknown or flensing out a whale carcass in a choppy sea with sharks circling, hoping for a bite of dinner?"

Discussing the pros and cons of each situation provided conversation and a distraction from the biting cold while they crossed the river, which was close to three-quarters of a mile wide. They survived the night by building a makeshift shelter with their knife and a borrowed ax.

Over the next several months, they made their way another two hundred and fifty miles west to an area near present-day Omaha, known as "Winter Quarters." The children suffered the most. The two youngest boys of Joseph and Ann Eliza's died, and a daughter that was born lived less than a year. During that winter, Joseph became more determined to find means to provide better food, clothing, and shelter for his family. So did George. The two men often talked for hours of their shared goal and ways to achieve it. The flight from Nauvoo had been hard on the thousands who made their way to Winter Quarters. Some abandoned the church and headed back east to rejoin other family members. Many died, but the majority gathered in and around Winter Quarters and began building substantial housing and planting crops as soon as spring arrived.

CHAPTER 17

Joseph swung the borrowed ax up to his shoulder as he and George finished some improvements they were making to each of their shelters. The effort was to make them more rain-tight and prepare them for a more comfortable winter, which was still a few months away. The families had taken several months since leaving Nauvoo to arrive in the Winter Quarters area in present-day Nebraska. The shelters (calling them houses would be an exaggeration) were an improvement to existing unprotected in the elements. It was July, and after fighting off freezing to death for weeks, Joseph enjoyed having the sweat roll off his face and soak his shirt while they were working.

"I'm not sure I'll ever warm up," Joseph commented to George. "We'd better return the ax then pick a few beans from the garden for supper on the way home." The summer was far enough along to allow them to add a little fresh produce to their diet.

"I can taste them now," replied George. "We can check to see if we can also pick some peas and radishes."

The two approached a man who was milking his cow. "Thanks for the use of the ax, Brother Jones," Joseph said as he swung the ax into a log next to a small pile of wood.

The man acknowledged the return of the borrowed tool, and then as the men were turning to leave, he said, "Have you heard who's here meeting with Brother Young?" The men stopped and swung around to hear this latest piece of news. "Captain Allen of the US Army. The United States has declared war with Mexico, and he wants several hundred men to volunteer for a year to march south and make a show of force."

"How could they possibly ask that of us after they've turned a blind eye to all the violence and persecution we've just endured? We've been driven from our homes and forced to leave our property, to head out unassisted across the mountains. And now they want us to help them fight a war?" Joseph was incredulous.

What Joseph started, George continued, his face flushed red with emotion. "Is there no end to being beat up and pushed around?" Both men were irritated to the point of not being able to stand still. They paced back and forth, shaking their heads and clenching their fists.

As the brother stood up from milking the cow and walked over to the other two, he added, "I know it seems like the universe is piling on and conspiring against us, but Brother Young said this could be a blessing in disguise."

The two men stopped cold and, with puzzled looks on their faces, said in unison, "How could this possibly be a blessing?"

"They'll pay us," replied the brother, "in advance." This immediately got their attention, and they asked for more details. "The volunteers will be paid soldiers' pay. Plus they'll be issued a rifle, a uniform, and other camping gear for the march. And they'll be allowed to keep it after they're discharged. Brother Young sees this as a way to help get us out west." Now the men had something to think about. It was no secret the church leaders were grappling with how to move thousands of nearly destitute families across rugged, mostly uncharted territory. Joseph and George had already discussed their circumstances and that they would probably have to wait two or more years to accumulate enough supplies before making the trip. The travel from Nauvoo had made it very clear they needed to be better prepared before moving on.

The discussion that evening with their wives was energetic, to put it mildly. It alternated between a recital of all the abuse they had been subjected to and the need for additional funds the church was being offered. The scriptural admonition to "turn the other cheek" and "forgive your enemies" entered into the discussion. After a thorough airing of all sides, they decided to retire, with no real decision as to which side they were on. Sleep did not come easily, as they all continued to play the arguments over and over in their minds.

CHAPTER 18

"I'll volunteer," said George the next morning. Joseph was shocked. Before he could say anything, George continued, "It makes sense. If Brigham Young is recommending we do this, I'm much younger than you and will be able to handle the long march better, and there may be fighting. Besides, I'm tougher and a better shot." Joseph feigned being insulted and started a wrestling match to show George just who was tougher. After several minutes, with both men gasping for breath lying on the ground, George continued. "You'll have to promise me you'll look after my family as if they are your own. Who knows where we'll meet back up? It may be after you've settled in the mountains. But I'll get there as soon as I can." Joseph agreed. Similar promises were being made all over the settlement as over five hundred men agreed to leave their families in the care of others. Within a few days, the group known as the Mormon Battalion marched off to Fort Leavenworth to be outfitted. Then they continued south to travel along near what was to become the US border with Mexico and finally to San Diego.

Several months later, Joseph was sitting in front of a pile of various vegetables, a few fruits, and grains in a cellar he had dug to keep their stores of food through the winter. There was also a side of venison he'd killed and skinned. They appeared to be better prepared for the coming cold season than they had been since leaving the Reeves farm. The question was, Would there be enough to get them not only through the winter but through a summer of travel to the West, plus through another winter before they could plant and raise more crops? As he mentally added up the amount of supplies needed, he felt a wave of depression creep into his mind. The harvest had been good, but he realized it would take several years to accumulate enough so that his family, and now also George's family, could expect to make the trip west. He and Ann Eliza already had lost three children to sickness, exposure, and lack of sufficient food. He was determined not to let that happen again.

That night, Joseph sat down with Ann Eliza and Mary to discuss their current situation, what they would need before they migrated, and plans to accumulate the needed supplies. The task looked daunting. But the discussion ended on an upbeat note, with all agreeing to look forward to a new home in the mountains.

The long winter had given ample time for lengthy discussions within the church leadership as to whether they should go all the way to the Pacific Ocean or stop somewhere in the Rocky Mountains. Several men had come through who had come from the Pacific coast. Their arguments to go there were quite compelling—mild climate, longer growing season, plenty of fishing and hunting. And there were also settlements at a few places along the coast. The settlements were a deterrent from going there. After the problems with the settlers at Kirkland, Ohio, Far West Missouri, and Nauvoo, the church leaders wanted a place that was completely their own, where there were no previous settlers. They wouldn't discourage others from moving there, but they wanted to be there first. That fact alone would go a long way in ensuring there wouldn't be a repeat of what had happened in Nauvoo, Far West, and Kirkland.

The first group to leave for the West started their journey the next spring in early April 1847. It was about 150 people, mostly men. Their goal was to decide on the location for the rest of the pioneers, establish a settlement, plant crops if there was time, and return. Then the next spring and summer, they would lead a larger group to the new settlement. Joseph set his sights on being ready to be in that group the next year. They were excited to see the first group go as he, Ann Eliza, and Mary set their minds to preparing for the journey.

A few weeks later, a small sick detachment from the Mormon Battalion met up with the first group as they were en route. Three men were sent back to the Winter Quarters camp to report details of the battalion. One of the arriving men spoke to Joseph about George. He reported George had become sick and was with the detachment when they started out. But along the trail, George had become so sick that he couldn't travel and was left with some trappers who had a cabin. Later, another small group of sick men from the battalion met up with the trappers where George had been left. They said George had died. When the trappers were pressed for details of George's last days and where he was buried, they were overly ambiguous. A search for the location of the grave turned up nothing.

Joseph returned to tell Mary the news. His feet felt like lead; every step was a real effort. On hearing the news, Mary's mind shut down. She withdrew and spent the next two months in bed. Ann Eliza was near her side most of the time. Gradually her animation returned as she accepted the realization she would be going to and living in the mountains without a husband. Joseph repeated the promise he had made to George, to care for her and her son. This helped Mary a bit, but the fact that she was now a widow at such a young age was a hard adjustment. She seriously considered returning east to where her parents lived and discussed this in detail with Ann Eliza and Joseph. The distance back to the East Coast was farther than to the mountains. To the West, the trail was barely made and troublesome. The roads to the East were well established. However, she would be traveling through an area that had driven them out and was unfriendly. Being a widowed mother with a young child, this gave her great concern. By continuing west, she was with like-minded people who cared for her. She had a lot of confidence in Joseph's ability to provide and watch out for them. She grudgingly opted to continue west.

Ann Eliza and Joseph saw that this could turn her bitter toward the church, and they tried to treat her whole situation with caution, tenderness, and understanding. At times, she would be so distraught she would take her son and go live with another family in the settlement, Ann Eliza and Joseph assumed. This caused them a lot of worry, but they could understand her need to be away from family for a time and opted just to make it clear to her that she always had a place at their table and in their home. But when and how much was her decision. The grief from losing George slowly abated over the next several months.

Joseph was always mindful of his promise to George to care for his family. He also realized the survival of the whole group depended mostly on him. The memory of being cold and hungry with sick and dying children was always on his mind. "I want to go west as bad as ever," he would tell Ann Eliza, "but I want to be sure we're prepared. We'd better wait another year." Each year, the disappointment was mitigated by the fact that they were making progress. They had acceptable shelter and were among their friends. As it turned out, it would be several years before Joseph would be ready to make the trip.

There always was a question in their minds as to whether George really died of sickness or if the men had killed him for the few items he had in his possession—a rifle, a knife, and his uniform. If he had died of sickness, the decent thing to do would be to save those items to send back to his family.

The rest of the report from the sick detachment about the battalion was good. They'd had no fighting against the Mexican Army, and, other than questionable treatment from the army doctor who was traveling with them and the normal rigors of a long march through wilderness, they were proceeding quite well.

Just before winter, the church leaders returned with the news that they had settled in the Great Basin near the Great Salt Lake. They were very pleased with the location. This would launch the Mormon Migration. Over seventy thousand people would make the journey over the next twenty years.

When spring arrived, Joseph made another critical assessment of how much of their supplies they had consumed over the winter and how much was left. Going to Salt Lake with the next group was out of the question. They had consumed more than he had expected, probably to regain some of the muscle and stamina sacrificed over several years of limited food. He felt they were in better health and better condition than they had been for years. Each year, near the end of February, he took an inventory of their food and other items to determine if they could make the trip to Salt Lake that summer. And each year they made some progress but not enough. It was difficult to see groups assemble and then watch them disappear over the western horizon.

Word would filter back that the Salt Lake settlement was growing and becoming more established. Streets and homestead lots were surveyed. Irrigation ditches were dug. A location for a new temple had been selected. Church members arrived from the eastern part of the United States and Europe, mostly Great Britain.

A girl and a boy had been born, but the baby girl died in her first year. Six babies had been born to Joseph and Ann Eliza, with only three surviving. With each child, Joseph couldn't help but feel he had failed as a provider and protector. And with each birth and death, he resolved to do better. The ache to head west was intense, but it made sense for them to stay where they were and continue to improve their resources and not be too anxious to leave. There were stories of families who were not sufficiently prepared and suffered greatly, and many deaths resulted. Each year the decision to wait another season or to leave was a life-and-death decision. Those who were prepared and left in early spring made the trip in good condition. Those who were ill prepared or left late in the season suffered.

CHAPTER 19

It would take six years from the time Joseph and his families arrived at Winter Quarters until he felt they were finally prepared sufficiently to strike out to the West. In discussions with Ann Eliza and Mary in January 1852, the decision was made. Barring sickness, accident, or other complication, they would set their efforts toward traveling to Salt Lake in the spring. Joseph had spent the fall and winter, when weather permitted, building a covered wagon. They had worked on an elaborate list of supplies to be included. Once they had the list close to final form, they could lay out how the wagon was to be packed, including what needed to be inside the wagon out of the rain and what could be fastened to the outside of the wagon. Their party would consist of three adults, Joseph, Ann Eliza, and Mary, and four children, eleven-, four-, and one-year-old boys of Joseph and Ann Eliza, and an eight-year-old boy of Mary. It was a big group. They needed to pack all their earthly possessions, plus enough supplies for the trip and to get them through the next winter and part of a growing season until more could be raised the next summer. But the size of the group was typical for those making the trip. Joseph took some comfort in the fact that thousands had preceded them and thousands would follow.

An advantage to having waited five years after the initial group before making the trip themselves was that the Salt Lake settlement was established, and crops had been raised and accumulated. So there was some extra to be shared with each season's new, arriving pioneers until they could raise their own stores of food. At least this is what Joseph had learned from meetings with those who had returned from Salt Lake to lead more groups west.

On a late winter, early spring day, Joseph was a few hundred feet from the shelter, looking closely for any sign of grass growing. He came to a ravine with a steep, south-facing bank. The dirt was soft and quite dry where it had sloughed off and dried in the increasing sunlight. It was sheltered from the wind. The sky was blue, and the sun was bright. Joseph couldn't help but lie down right on the dirt, stare up at the sky, and savor the warm sun. It was a mini-celebration of surviving through one more, cold, gray, depressingly drab winter. It still froze at night. There were only a few minutes each day that were warm enough to start forcing away the effects of the winter. It was still too cold for insects to be out. There were not many birds yet either, only a few eagles, hawks, and ravens. Joseph closed his eyes and breathed in deeply, smelling the early spring smells, which were mostly drying dirt and sagebrush.

Just then, he heard Ann Eliza call his name from the shelter. He crawled up the bank until his head was high enough that he could see her at the door. He waved and called back, asking her to come to him. A minute later, she appeared at the top of the bank. He motioned to an area where she could come down the bank.

"Come sit with me a few minutes," he said. "It's so pleasant down here out of the wind." He helped her down and motioned to a spot where they could both sit. Neither of them gave any thought to sitting on the bare dirt, just so it wasn't mud. Ann Eliza, being raised on a farm, and Joseph, working with Mr. Reeves several years on the farm, had a real appreciation for good dirt that was fertile and ready to grow anything planted in it.

"I was just sitting here out of the wind, enjoying the sun when you called. I know it's been a few months since we decided we would go west this year. I still think we'll make the trip this year. How about you?"

"I feel the same way," she replied. Then after a pause, she added, "And I'm quite sure Mary does too. But it's almost a shame to leave what we have here. The shelter is quite comfortable after years of chinking up the holes and digging a cellar to store food and building a corral for the oxen." Joseph had bargained several years ago for a couple of newborn calves in trade for helping a neighbor plant and harvest his crops. He raised those calves specifically to pull the wagon he had built over this past winter. He also knew he would probably have to butcher them on their arrival in Salt Lake to feed his family through the following winter. He tried not the think of that since he had grown fond of them over the years. As soon as the roads were dry enough, he would train them to pull his wagon, first empty and then gradually with more and more weight.

"We've been here the longest since we got married and developed quite the homestead," Joseph answered. "It'll be a shame to leave it. But look at it this way: it'll make a great place for someone new who's making their way from England to Salt Lake. Wouldn't it have been nice if someone had left a homestead for us when we came from Nauvoo?" They both nodded as they recalled the first few years of struggle and the death of three of their children.

Joseph got up early and traveled to the church office to put his name on the list to join a group intending to travel to the Great Basin this season. It was early April. They wouldn't leave until June, but the church office was buzzing and crowded from morning till past dark each day. Thousands had already made the trip, and the trail was well established. But even as thousands had left for Salt Lake, thousands more had arrived from the East, wanting to make the trip. Most of the travelers had to do as Joseph had done; they had to wait until they could afford a wagon, team, and supplies. Dozens of little communities were built around Winter Quarters as they farmed and built up their supplies for the journey.

It felt good to have been in one place this long. They were all anxious to go west, but at the same time, they knew it would be a challenge. The decision to continue west was not taken lightly. Joseph felt the added pressure of his promise to George Coleman to watch after Mary and her son and the added supplies that would require. The list at the travel office was already several hundred long and was growing every day. This year was shaping up to be the largest number of travelers yet. *More safety in numbers*, Joseph thought.

CHAPTER 20

On June 5, 1852, Joseph and Ann Eliza were lying in bed trying, unsuccessfully, to go to sleep. The wagon was packed, for the fourth time. Both were reviewing for the thousandth time if they had everything. This would be their last night to sleep in a comfortable bed for several months. They had no delusions as to what lay ahead—dry, dusty, tedious, day-after-day monotony, filled with mind-numbing boredom, punctuated with occasional episodes of jaw-clenching panic as Indians showed up demanding something unattainable or else threatening life and limb.

Joseph suddenly sat up and said something that had been nibbling around the edges of both their thoughts now for months. "Why are we doing this? We've built a nice homestead here with corrals and a storage cellar. Can't we serve the Lord just as well from here, helping others get outfitted and organized to make the trek?"

Ann Eliza sat up herself but didn't say anything for a minute as she reviewed in her mind, again, the pros and cons of making this trip. "Strictly from a logic point of view, it makes sense to stay here. Why subject ourselves and our family to the hardships and unknown danger when we have achieved good stability here?" she argued. But as they looked at each other in the pale light of the night, they both knew the answer. She finally said, "Staying here just doesn't feel right. Going to Salt Lake does."

Joseph nodded and continued, "It's the next step of our story, our mission, our reason for being brought this far. You have to do what feels right. Like the day I ran away from home in England and slipped aboard a whaling ship. Looking back at it, it was like jumping off a cliff in the dark, not knowing how far down the ground was or if I would land in soft dirt or on rock. You do it because you feel an urging, it's something that needs to be done. So … let's do it!"

Joseph woke a least a dozen times through the night. It was a fitful sleep. Finally, at about four o'clock, he got up, dressed, and went out to feed and water the oxen, waking the others as he walked out the door. At seven o'clock, all were loaded in the wagon. They had traveled a grand fifty feet when he stopped, turned to the others, and said, "Let's sing a song," and he started "Praise to the Man." The others, caught off guard by his singing, finally joined in about the third line. By the end of the verse, they had all joined in and were making a fair amount of noise. "Hallelujah!" Joseph shouted as he pulled off his hat and waved it in the air. "We're on our way." That gave an air of celebration to the event, and they took their place in line along with more than eighty other wagons. The cut-off number for the size of this company was 250 people. But as was often the case, a few indecisive family members decided to join up with the rest of their family at the last minute, so the final number was close to 290.

Their goal was to travel fifteen miles a day. The first few days were far below that number as men and animals learned what would be the general routine for the next several months. Women and children also had to learn the routine of rising early enough to get the children dressed, fed, and the inevitable scratches and scraps doctored. Those fortunate enough to have a milk cow included getting the cow milked and the milk put in the milk keg on the wagon. By the end of the day, they could retrieve a ball of butter to add to a biscuit, which would raise the energy level for the day.

CHAPTER 21

On the fourteenth day out, about midafternoon, Joseph was having trouble staying awake. Their boy Billy, actually William Reeves Godfrey, was on "buffalo chip" assignment. Firewood was proving to be scarce. In this area, there was no wood for cooking fires, so they resorted to what previous companies had learned to do, cook with dried buffalo chips. Buffalo chips were buffalo manure that had been left by the many animals in the area. It had dried in the sun to a stiff, pie-shaped piece of digested grass. This initially shocked and disgusted the Godfreys and most of the travelers. Most of the protein and other nutrients were extracted as it passed through the gut of the animals, leaving woody, burnable residue when dried. In fact, they had a special bucket that hung on the outside of the wagon. Anyone and everyone who encountered a chip was to pick it up and throw it in the bucket until the bucket was full. Sometimes days would go by without passing enough trees to supply fuel for the cooking fires. With a full chip bucket, they always had something they could burn. The massive buffalo herds had grown, so now, at this critical time in American history, they provided not only walking food for the migrating travelers but fuel to cook the meat with.

Previous pioneers had even developed a special way to build a chip-cooking fire. They would dig a hole about eight inches in diameter, and two smaller holes next to it with a passageway into the larger hole. Then they would put one or two chips in the large hole to burn. They could then set the cooking pan over the fire, supported by the ground. Air was supplied through the smaller side holes. This proved to be a simple yet efficient way to utilize the chips and provide fuel for the thousands of cooking fires.

It was Billy's assignment to search the ground they covered for buffalo chips. He had strict instructions never to be more than one rod away from the wagon should wolves or Indians suddenly show up. "What's a rod?" he asked Joseph when first given the assignment.

"It's a little over sixteen feet," responded Joseph. "Here, I'll show you," he said as he walked away from Billy about a rod. "It's about that far. Be sure you are never farther away from the wagon than this in case trouble suddenly shows up. And remember, if we can't find any firewood, we'll only have the buffalo chips to cook our supper. Without them, we go to bed hungry." Joseph had learned to explain not only what to do and how to do it but why it needed to be done. At age eleven, Billy was nearly a man and would soon have all the responsibilities of a man. Billy and Moroni, Mary's son with George Coleman, were good friends most of the time. At other times they were rivals. They would compete for who could run the fastest, who could throw a knife the farthest and have it stick point-first in a log, and even with household chores such as cleaning the rotten fruits and vegetables out of the cellar in the spring. Billy, being three years older than Moroni, usually won any contest, but that didn't stop Moroni from always nipping at his heels.

There were two other children of Joseph and Ann Eliza in the group. George was age four, named after George Coleman, who had died while with the Mormon Battalion, and one-year-old Joseph, named after his dad. Mary was an independent person. She exhibited that independence by trying not to rely solely on Joseph to provide for her. She made a point of making other friends and became involved in their activities and interests. But when it came time to leave Winter Quarters, she had no choice but to latch onto Joseph's group. Joseph understood she and Moroni were a family. However, he made it clear, as gently as possible, that she was welcome as part of his group. He had promised George he would care for them, and he was prepared to do so. But it was her choice. Being a young, widowed mother launching out on a 1,100-mile journey into the wilds was not for the faint of heart. Nor was it an easy decision for her. What made it even more difficult was the resentment she felt for being a young, widowed mother in this position. She battled these feelings and was often tempted to curse God for taking George from her. But she wasn't the only one in this predicament. Due to the persecution of being forced from their homes, many had lost husbands and other family members to the mobs and sickness that ensued, being exposed to the harsh weather and lack of food. There wasn't a family at Winter Quarters that hadn't lost someone in the effort to live what they believed and reach their valley of sanctuary.

Joseph was sleepy because it had been his turn to take the second shift of the night watch. Indians had been sighted the day before. One of their favorite ploys was to hide in the brush on the fringe of the area where the stock had been turned out for the night, until the cattle got used to their faint scent and wandered close to where they were hiding. Then they would quietly spook one or two of the animals farther and farther away from the herd until they could get away with them. The loss of even one animal had a major impact on the company. Thus, they always had guards at night.

On this day, Joseph was near the front of the company when a pair of scouts came galloping in, raising a few eyebrows. "Everyone, pay attention. There could be trouble," Joseph alerted all in his group. He couldn't hear what was being said over the noise of the wagon wheels, but it looked like good news rather than bad. A few minutes later, word spread down the line of wagons that a herd of buffalo had been sighted. The riders had come back to enlist a couple of the assigned hunters who had horses and rifles to ride out and kill a couple of the animals. Two animals would feed the entire company for a couple of days. But in the warm weather, which was getting warmer by the day, they couldn't keep the meat. The company was under strict instructions to kill only what they could consume. No wasting the meat.

As the hunters rode out, the wagons continued to plod along the trail. Joseph walked to the top of a small hill in the direction of the herd to see if he could see the hunt take place. As he reached the top of the hill, about another half mile away, Joseph couldn't believe what he saw. There were thousands—no, tens of thousands—of buffalo milling around the prairie, grazing on the tufts of grass. Joseph couldn't see the end of the herd. The two riders rode to within fifty yards of the animals, each firing once while they sat on their horses, downing two buffalo. As one rider began skinning the animals, the other rode back to the company to have a wagon come haul the meat back.

That evening, the two carcasses were located near the center of the camp. Each captain of ten was sent to pick up a section of the meat and distribute it to their group. No one in Joseph's group had eaten buffalo before. While at Winter Quarters, rabbit, squirrel, grouse, the occasional deer, and even doves had been eaten whenever they could get them. But a buffalo was bigger than Joseph had dare shoot, realizing that shooting the animal was only the beginning. It would then need to be dressed or gutted, which was intimidating to begin with, and then cut up and processed, meaning preserved in some way to delay spoilage. This could be done by drying the meat or salting the meat or smoking it. Smoking the meat meant cooking it by exposing it to the hot, heavy, dense smoke of burning wood, usually oak or pine in a permanent kiln. A kiln is not something they traveled with. Cutting up a large dead animal was something Joseph had seen many times. But a buffalo on the high plains was very different from a whale in the ocean.

The company was grateful for the opportunity for any meat to add some extra protein and energy to their diet. They even caught as many juices and drippings as they could from the meat and mixed it with some flour to make a simple gravy, getting all the value they could from the meat. The next day, the company felt a real boost, both from the extra protein and from better sleep, resulting from having fuller bellies.

CHAPTER 22

"Ann Eliza ... Ann Eliza ... Ann Eliza," Joseph repeated in a soft, mellow voice, as mellow as one could have at five in the morning.

Something must be wrong, Ann Eliza thought to herself. *Or else he wouldn't be trying to wake me up*, her thought continued. Mustering every ounce of strength to stoke the fires of logical thought out of the misty, velvet, cozy mental retreat she had lapsed into, she barely moved her lips. "What is it, Joseph?"

"It's time to get up," he said softly.

That can't be right. I haven't even got to sleep yet, she mentally argued with this voice that was intruding on her bliss. But she knew it was a losing argument, and ever so gradually, she began the mental calisthenics of reviewing the previous day's events and what chores must be done in the next few minutes and hours. The previous day had been a hard day. The trail was flat, but it was quite sandy. The narrow wheels cut easily into the sand several inches. That gave the effect of always trying to climb a steep hill as the wheels tried to climb out of the sand. They had only made eight miles, roughly half of what their target was each day. They were exhausted, and as soon as they finished up the day, they fell into bed. Finishing the day included finding enough feed for the oxen, building a fire and cooking something to fill their belly's, cleaning the dishes, and putting out the bedrolls.

Ann Eliza usually rode in the wagon. But when they needed to lighten the wagon as much as possible, no one rode. Joseph would be up by the oxen, giving them verbal encouragement, even pulling on them most of the time, while Ann Eliza, Mary, and the boys walked behind and often pushed. Joseph had never heard of Isaac Newton nor his law of inertia, but Joseph knew the principle well. "An object in motion tends to stay in motion. An object at rest tends to stay at rest." *Keep the wagon moving if at all possible. Once the wagon stops, it is twice as hard to get moving again, especially if mired in mud or sand.*

No one knew the effort it took to get the group ready to travel better than Joseph. And even though the previous day had been as hard for him as anyone, he only had half the sleep. Last night was another night for him to put in a shift of guarding the livestock. Wolves and Indians were always a threat. Occasional gunfire was heard during the night when the guard saw or heard something that indicated something or someone was nearby, waiting for a chance to drive off an animal. A shot fired in the general direction of the intruder let him know the guard was armed and would protect their property if needed. Unless more shots were fired, the camp didn't respond.

More likely, a small group of Indians would approach the company during the day and demand something in exchange for allowing the travelers to cross their land. They were usually offered some meat if they had extra, or salt, or perhaps a piece of fabric or beads. Rarely were the Indians satisfied, and it usually took some firm words before the Indians left.

The general routine was to get up at five, have breakfast, tend to the animals, and be ready to travel by seven. Most days were mind-numbingly boring and tedious. On this day, about midday, they came to a small stream. It would be easy to cross, but it was big enough to supply ample water for the stock and filling of the water kegs on the wagons. It was also a chance for a bath or at least a good wash up if you were so inclined, which most were. The company captain, David Wood, directed they should make use of the stream and have some food during the break. A small group of men walked downstream a few hundred yards and managed to dam up the stream or at least slow it down and deepen it to make it easier to wash. Joseph and a few other men walked a few hundred yards upstream and did the same thing for the women and children. This was the best they could do under the circumstances to allow some modestly. Most of the women were content just to wash hands and faces, while others who were bolder also washed feet, arms, faces, and their hair. A few of the men stripped completely, washed all over, and even rinsed out their underwear. After wringing out as much water as possible, the men would put the wet underwear back on and enjoy a little extra cooling as the fabric air-dried in the sun.

After the previous hard day and not fully waking up since morning, the dip in the stream provided some much-needed refreshing. The afternoon was hot and dusty as usual, but the stream gave Joseph a renewed surge of energy. Most of the time, no fire was built for lunch. Instead, they snacked on biscuits and previously cooked meat. During this stretch of the trail, they also found wild onions that were dug and eaten like apples. Since their choices of food items were limited, they tolerated several foods, like the onions, they wouldn't normally choose if they had a choice.

Since they had some downtime at the stream during the day, the company traveled longer into the evening than usual. In this area, the trail was hard, flat, and fairly easy to navigate. When the company finally did stop for the day, everyone scampered about, fixing a meager supper, tending to stock, preparing beds for the night, and trying to make the best use of what little light remained. Most were in bed before the bedtime bugle, which didn't seem to come quickly enough for most, especially Joseph, who had the late watch tonight. He would catch all the sleep he could till about one o'clock. Then he would rise and spend the rest of the night watching the stock for any signs of Indians, wolves, or bad weather.

CHAPTER 23

On the trail, Joseph had become the alarm clock for the group. For some reason, he found he woke up at the time he needed to get up, not necessarily *wanted* to get up but *needed* to get up. On most mornings, he arose earlier than the others, tended to the stock, and did anything else that didn't require everyone. Then as the eastern glow in the sky increased to the point of allowing one to see the surrounding wagons and terrain, he would wake the others as gently as he could and still convey enough urgency in the message to reanimate bodies that had become immobile.

"Ann Eliza ... Ann Eliza!" Joseph was calling her.

What could he want? I need some sleep, she thought to herself, not realizing it was time to get up already.

"Come here. You've got to see this!" Joseph urged.

Ann fought to clear her thoughts and bring her mental operation up to speed. She pulled herself out of bed and wandered, some might say staggered, to where Joseph was standing. He was pointing to the Northwest. She blinked her eyes a couple of times and scanned the landscape for what it was he was so excited about. It didn't take long. They had heard about it, but to see it in person, in the early morning with the sun rising, was beyond anything they had imagined. They thought it was about three miles away, but it was closer to ten miles. Before them, jutting out of the rolling hills stood Chimney Rock. The night before, they had been so preoccupied with the evening preparations, plus some low-hanging clouds obscuring the view, no one had noticed. But this morning, in the cool, clear air, nearly everyone in camp was oohing and awing over the view. After hundreds of miles of near flat prairie, this was striking! Many journal entries from previous companies had used the word "romantic" when writing about seeing Chimney Rock.

After several minutes of staring in preoccupied silence at the structure, Joseph commented, "I can see why previous companies have written about Chimney Rock. It is magnificent. But I'm not sure why they would call it romantic."

Ann Eliza responded, "The word romantic is related to love. Aren't we here because of love? Love of God. Love of the gospel. Love for each other and our children. The trail might be hard and troublesome, but I love the beauty of this new country we're seeing." That made sense to Joseph. She continued, "I also look at it as a monument to what we're doing, building God's kingdom. God put it in our path to cheer us on, to encourage us on this journey." Joseph had learned that Ann Eliza possessed, and often expressed, the tender feelings that he lacked, or perhaps had stifled through years of associating with sailors and other men whose main aim in life was to outdo the fellow standing next to him.

After nearly two months on the trail, Joseph realized that Chimney Rock was a preview, a mild preview of the rugged mountains they would see and need to cross before being able to rest near the Great Salt Lake.

The next night, they camped probably as close as they would be to Chimney Rock. The evening was spent viewing the mountain and commenting on everything from the type of rock it was to how it may have come into existence. Some amused themselves by discussing how many times lightning must strike it in a year. A few men jumped on horses and rode over to the base of the mountain to get a closer look.

Several days later, Ann Eliza asked Joseph, "Do you ever try to picture in your mind what the Great Salt Lake basin looks like?" They were no longer thinking about what they had left at Nauvoo and Winter Quarters and were focused forward, to what they were traveling toward. They were on a level stretch of trail where both were able to ride in the wagon. There were more rock outcroppings, or rock cliffs as many in the company called them. Regardless, the country they were traveling through now was a departure from the hundreds of miles of flat prairie they had traveled since leaving Winter Quarters. Not only were there rock formations, but the bluffs were higher, and the streams ran swifter, with steeper approaches and exits, all indicating steeper terrain. They had to double and triple team the wagons to get over ravines that crossed the trail.

"I've heard and talked to many who have been there. According to them, we've not seen anything yet," he replied.

"How can that be?" she said. "We have to double and triple team the wagons at times now. How could it be worse and still be passable?"

Joseph thought a minute. "The Saints have been making this trip now for five years. Some have made the trip several times. Whatever we encounter, just remember, it is possible." Joseph took a drink of water from a jug, then continued, "The mountains must be high, unbelievably high, but we don't go over the tops of the mountains. The road goes through the mountains, through passes between mountains. I know the first group, the first few groups, had to scout several different ways of getting into the basin. By now, the road is established, and many of the obstacles that were in their way in the beginning have been removed, or they've figured a way around them."

"What else have you heard?" probed Ann Eliza. This was an opportunity to discuss what they were doing, now that they were experiencing the trail, and details concerning their destination. It was a bit strange they hadn't discussed it before, but there were always more important things to take care of—things like getting some food prepared and eaten, then cleaning up, packing up the utensils and food, and getting ready to start traveling. They had to clean and bandage scrapes or other injuries by one of the boys, including Joseph. Oxen had to be hitched up or unhitched, led to grass or water, or doctored. Their survival and progress depended on a healthy team of oxen, and great efforts were expended by them, by everyone, to keep the teams healthy. There was milk to be put in the churning keg when they could get it, and meat to be cut up and preserved as much as possible. Joseph wasn't assigned as one of the hunters. He didn't have a horse and was content to share in the meat that was killed and brought back to camp. His main extra duty had been as a night guard. He preferred this, except for missing the much-needed sleep. The camp was usually quiet, and the night sky was amazing to watch. His experience as a whaler had made him an expert in finding the constellations and locating the North Star.

"We should be at Devil's Gate within a day or two," he continued.

"Devil's Gate?" said Ann Eliza. "That sounds a bit alarming."

"From what I understand," replied Joseph, "we don't go through it. It's a steep-sided V cut through a rock cliff by a stream. It sounds quite impressive from what I've heard. The elevation of Winter Quarters was about a thousand feet. I understand the Salt Lake's elevation is about four thousand feet."

"Elevation? What are you talking about?" quizzed Ann Eliza.

"It is how many feet above sea level the ground is," answered Joseph. Having spent several decades on the sea, this was an entirely new experience, and Joseph was quite curious about the elevation of where they were going. He'd specifically asked those returning from Salt Lake City about the elevation. "Through this stretch of road, we're at about five thousand feet."

"So it's downhill from here?" asked Ann Eliza, who was getting an education in topography.

"Sorry to disappoint you, but no, it's not. In fact, in a couple of weeks, we'll be crossing the Continental Divide, and that's over seven thousand feet."

Now her head was spinning as she tried to digest what Joseph had just told her. "We've been on the trail now about two months. And you're telling me we have to climb another two thousand feet before we start coming down?" Her question was not a question of alarm but one of amazement. It was probably better they hadn't talked about the details of the journey before. Now she understood why Joseph had taken this task so seriously, often wandering off to some secluded place to review and mull over in his mind just what they were about to do. She started to understand why he had been so careful to be prepared for the trip with food, clothes, oxen, and wagon. This is why he would sometimes hitch up the oxen and go find different streams to practice fording. The oxen handled very differently when there was water and mud to contend with. At the time, she couldn't understand why he was taking so much time driving the oxen in different conditions. He even went out several times in rain with thunder and lightning. This day she had an epiphany. She understood better than ever before that Joseph felt a genuine responsibility for the lives and well-being of all in their party, including Mary and her son, Moroni.

"What is the Continental Divide?" asked Ann Eliza. "It sounds like something I'm not sure I want to cross."

Joseph was enjoying sharing some of the knowledge he'd acquired over the last several years by talking with returning pioneers. "The Continental Divide is a range of mountains that runs north and south, generally. The water on the east side of the divide all ends up in the Atlantic Ocean while the water on the west side flows to the Pacific Ocean." Again, Ann Eliza nodded but took her time to consider this new information.

Over the next couple of weeks, as the mountains loomed higher around them, they were both awed and frightened—awed because neither had seen such rugged, rocky monuments of God's creativity and frightened by the fact that they were being expected to traverse such terrain. Echoing in their minds were the words that Joseph had so innocently recited, "Some have made this trip several times. Whatever we encounter, just remember, it is possible."

The next night, in the middle of the night, Joseph finished an early watch duty and slipped into bed next to Ann Eliza. She mumbled something to acknowledge him being there and then was back into a deep slumber. Joseph, however, was not as quick to drift off. A little excitement near the end of his watch had his mind racing, and it would take longer for him to settle into sleep. It was a full moon, but there were enough clouds so the night alternated between nearly pitch black and the pale, gray outlines of objects as the uncovered moon lit up the countryside. He was scanning slowly right and left as he watched the stock, some continuing to eat and others lying down for the night. Then out of the corner of his eye, he thought he saw something move behind a large rock. He focused instantly on that area, looking for some additional movement. Not seeing anything but hearing a faint rustle that seemed out of place, he reached down and picked up a rock about the size of a grapefruit. He threw it in a high arch in the direction of the boulder. He would have been justified in shooting his gun but was reluctant to do so, not wanting to alarm the camp if what he saw turned out to be nothing. The flying rock crashed into the boulder and ricocheted between two ridges on the rock, amplifying the noise. *If anything is there, that should scare them out,* he thought to himself. He watched around the boulder closely for any sign of movement. After fifteen, maybe twenty, seconds, behind the boulder about fifty feet, again on the edge of his focus, he saw quick movement next to the ground. Then it disappeared behind some large sagebrush. Joseph couldn't tell if it was human or an animal. It could have been either. He was now on high alert. He raised his gun and walked a few yards toward the boulder. Regardless of what it was, he wanted to appear aggressive to let it be known he meant to protect what was his. He kept walking, looking right and left, but nothing else turned up. After thirty minutes, the next guard came out to relieve him. Joseph explained what had just happened to the new guard. Then he headed back to the wagon.

He heard Ann Eliza's deep breathing, indicating she was relaxed and in a deep sleep. He thought of how deeply he cared for her. And not far off were his three boys, whom he prized. *How many women would be willing to leave the safety and security of established parents and a solid home life to go into the wilderness, to where there were no guarantees, only hopes of the type of life they sought?* he thought. He was also amazed at his circumstances in life, from the home of an abusive drunk, to a whaler sailing all over the world, to a father with a family seeking a life in a mountainous wilderness he had never seen. He had been penniless several times. Now look at him. Not that he was rich in material things, but he had a sufficient amount to pack up and journey to the Great Basin. And he had the richness of his family and his faith. As these feelings washed over him, so did a feeling of sweet confidence that what they were doing was the right thing. But lingering in all this emotion was also the ache for those children they had lost. He felt he had failed them, failed to provide sufficiently, failed to protect them from exposure to the harsh things of this world, failed to keep them strong and healthy. He resolved, for the thousandth time, he would do better. After all, he had done the best he could under the circumstances. But that was small consolation for the loss he now felt at their absence. Things were better now and would continue to get better when they got to Salt Lake. He was on the road to making a good life better. It was a sublime feeling of deep gratitude for what he had, mixed with bold confidence in where he was going. He was happy!

CHAPTER 24

"Bro Woods wants to have a meeting with all the captains, hunters, and guards tonight before bedtime," Joseph explained to Ann Eliza as they worked at setting up camp and preparing supper. It was not unusual to have such meetings as they approached some danger or event or change in the trail conditions. The meeting would include most of the heads of families, and Joseph expected it was to inform them of the terrain they could expect from here to the basin. They had passed Devil's Gate and were approaching South Pass, which was the Continental Divide. The trail had changed from generally flat, soft, sandy, and boggy in some places to hard, rocky, and steep. The wagons required repairs more often, and wheels needed to be tightened and adjusted. Several wagon axles in the company had snapped due to the increasingly rough and rocky trail, requiring major downtime as new hardwood was located, a log cut, and the new axle carved from the log. The majority of the company moved on after a new log was secured, leaving a small party of two or three wagons to carve, fit, and attach the new axle, then travel extra-long days to catch up to the main party. Joseph easily had the skill to help carve a new axle but hadn't been asked to stay behind because he had two women and four young children in his group.

Joseph helped get the kids settled down for the night and then made his way to the centerfire where the meeting was to be held and found a good place to sit. After a few deep breaths, he could feel the tension of the day leave his body, and in less than two minutes, he was fighting to stay awake, waiting for the start of the meeting.

"Brethren," Captain Woods began, "I'll keep this a short as possible, but I just wanted to make everyone aware of what to expect between here and the basin. Perhaps tomorrow or the next day, we'll cross the Continental Divide. I know that sounds like it will be hard, but that part is not difficult at all, like crossing the top of a mild, rounded hill. It's what comes later that we need to be prepared for. "From here to the basin are several narrow, rocky, steep canyons. We need to be always alert and aware of your children, the cattle, and what condition your wagon is in. Be sure everything on and in your wagon is secure each morning before you begin. And if something comes loose during the day, stop immediately and secure it. If you don't secure it immediately, it will likely cause further damage and cause more delay. We need to pay extra attention to the weather. Should a thunderstorm occur while we're traveling a narrow canyon, the creek could easily rise enough in a short time to carry off a wagon or stock or even one of the children. We sent a message ahead yesterday by express rider to President Young. This was to report our location, condition, and expected arrival. Those of you with family already in the basin will generally know when to expect you."

This last statement got Joseph to thinking, *Who knows we're coming? And where will we settle when we get there?* Not that he was worried; he, or they, just hadn't given it much thought before now. The main objective of "getting there" was always the focus. Would they dare to start thinking about what life would be like once they got there? As the meeting ended and the crowd began to disperse, Joseph wandered back to the wagon with overwhelming thoughts about their arrival, which was now just three to five weeks away and a near certainty.

"How was the meeting?" asked Ann Eliza as he neared the wagon. She expected the usual casual response but instead got a penetrating, wide-eyed answer.

"I think we're going to make it!" exclaimed Joseph.

"I never doubted you'd get us there," she replied. "You seem surprised."

"I guess I'd been concentrating so much on having everything prepared, me being prepared, then just getting through each day, that

I'd never given any thought to actually being there and living there." Joseph realized that by now there were probably over ten thousand people living in and around the basin with established lots and roads. It was quite a change from the empty wilderness of a few years before. As they fell into bed and he drifted off to sleep, he wondered just what he would do at his new home. Most everyone raised some crops and cattle or horses, but this was a new chapter. A clean sheet of paper. Maybe he'd look into picking up a trade like masonry, blacksmithing, or carpentry. He didn't have to decide tonight, but it was interesting to think about.

As they approached South Pass, anticipation grew as everyone looked forward to the milestone. The pass itself was quite mild, as far as ruggedness and steepness were concerned, but it was the dividing line between the eastern slope of the country and the western slope. What was noteworthy was the number of companies. All established routes to the West Coast went through the South Pass. Whether you were going to Oregon and the Willamette Valley, Salt Lake, and the Great Basin, the goldfields of Northern California, or the warm climate of Southern California, you went through South Pass. Tens of thousands had passed this area in the previous few years on their way to a new life.

When they camped near the pass, Joseph helped clean up after supper and put the kids to bed. As he looked ahead and behind on the trail, he could see hundreds of campfires of other companies who were in the same area. An eerie feeling came over him—not that he was alarmed but because it had been months since being around so many people.

"I think I'll walk down the trail a bit to see what I can find out from another company," he said to Ann Eliza as she mended a hole that had appeared in one of the boy's britches that day.

"Don't be long. The lights-out bugle is due shortly," she replied.

Joseph walked down the trail about a quarter mile. As he approached the first campfire of another company, it was just after sundown. At first, he was more interested in observing than talking, so he stayed far enough away so as not to be noticed but close enough to hear some of what was said. Even though they were technically outside the United States, memories of being driven from Nauvoo were foremost in his mind. He had heard there were companies from Illinois on the trail, and several from Missouri as well. He wasn't sure if he would be more nervous about being around them or they would be more nervous about being around him. As he walked slowly but steadily past the camp, he noticed it was probably two families around this campfire—two moms, two dads, and six, no seven children. There was the usual expected talk of trail conditions, of having to live out of a cramped covered wagon, of mosquitoes and the normal squabbles between the kids and between kids and parents. There was no indication of where they were from or their destination. Joseph kept walking. The next campfire was just women and a few children. The men could easily be out with the stock or on their way back from doing some hunting. From the conversation he picked up at this campfire, he learned they were from St. Louis. He also heard complaints about the nice homes they had left and what they had now, definitely a step down from what they had been used to. He also learned they were headed for the Willamette Valley in Oregon. Doing some quick calculations, Joseph realized that company would be another three to four months on the trail. He shook his head as he realized they were in for some trying times, especially with the attitude he heard from them. There was no question that spending four to six months on the trail was only for the most determined and stouthearted folks. As he turned and headed back toward his wagon, he silently gave thanks for his family and their resolve to reach their new home. It hadn't been easy, but a contrary attitude would easily double the difficulty.

"What did you find out?" asked Ann Eliza as he approached the wagon and she put the final stitches on her mending.

"I learned I've got the best wife and family a guy could have." He wrapped his arms around her in a big hug and gave her a solid kiss on the mouth.

"Joseph! The kids aren't asleep yet," she gasped.

"It'll do 'em good to know their dad loves their mother. Besides that, I learned the next camp is trying to get to the end of the trail just like us. Now let's go to bed before there's not enough night left to make it worthwhile." Joseph put out the fire, crawled under the blanket, and was asleep in less than two minutes.

CHAPTER 25

The company was on the trail early. They had become quite efficient at getting up, eating, cleaning up, gathering up, and starting the day's normal boring trek to reach their mileage goal. But today would be a bit different, and most in the company anticipated some mild excitement. They were to start down Echo Canyon today, thus named by previous companies for its narrow trail and sheer rock sides that had the effect of echoing and magnifying every sound as they passed through it. When they started down the canyon, an unusual hush fell over the company. They were startled by how normal conversations were amplified. It was like every thought, every comment, every directive, and every criticism was shared with the whole company. Even the stock seemed to walk quietly and tiptoe along. Then it slowly became a novelty. As they grew more accustomed to the effect, some started sharing thoughts and feelings. "Hooray for Israel!" someone called from several hundred yards away. Followed by, "It's a beautiful day." Then someone else called, "It's great to be alive!" Then the younger generation got into the excitement. "Henry loves Patty," and "I want roast buffalo for dinner." It was as if everyone in the company was given a megaphone for a short time and could express whatever was rolling around in his or her head at that moment to the hundreds who were on the trail.

"This will be one of those times," Joseph said as they were gathered around the fire, eating supper after a day that was notable and memorable.

"One of *those* times?" asked Ann Eliza to goad Joseph into a more elaborate explanation.

"Another week or two, and we'll be in the basin at the end of a journey we started years ago in New Jersey when we gave a hiker on the road a lift into town." Everyone was now mildly interested in what Joseph had to say. "George and I were taking a load of barley from Mr. Reeves's farm into town to trade for winter supplies. A few miles before town, we came upon a fellow walking along, also headed into town. We stopped and offered him a ride. It turned out he was a Mormon elder and started telling us about the church and the Book of Mormon."

The boys were mildly interested in the details since they hadn't heard this story before, but the women were eager for Joseph to get to his point. To appease everyone in the group, Joseph skipped lightly over the details that brought them to today. "We probably won't remember much about the last three months on the prairie. But from what I hear, the rest of the way into the basin will be hard." After a pause, he added, "And exhilarating. Going through Echo Canyon is something we'll always remember. Next we climb to the highest point on the trail, nearly 8,500 feet." Joseph could see the question on the boys' faces, so he added, "Eighty-five hundred feet above sea level." He was amused at watching the puzzled look turn into a look of understanding and then into a look of alarm.

"We're going to do what?" the boys asked in unison.

"This trip is about not only the number of miles we travel horizontally but also the number of feet vertically." Joseph enjoyed the next few minutes, explaining what he had learned over the last few years in preparing for this trip. He finished with, "I'm sure for the rest of our lives we'll tell our children and grandchildren about when we crossed the plains and came to the Great Salt Lake. Now we'd better get some sleep while we can. The next few days will be tough."

The next few days were tough. The climb to the top of "Big Mountain" was punishing. Each step was a climb higher. The air was thinner, and when they reached the top, they were gasping for breath. The oxen were gasping, their sides heaved, and sweat dripped from their bodies. The company leader wisely called for a two-hour break before starting down.

Traveling downhill turned out to be almost as tiring and challenging as the climb uphill. It took a different set of skills. The wagon had to be held back from racing over the top of the oxen and other wagons in front. Joseph kept his hand constantly on the yoke of the oxen, steadying them through this unusual circumstance. Constant pressure on the brake would quickly overheat the brake and wheel and cause failure. The oxen were coaxed into holding back instead of pulling. When the slope was too steep, men would chain the back wheels of the wagons so they wouldn't turn, causing them to skid down the mountain. The company traveled later than usual due to the long break at the top of the mountain. After crossing the summit, they had to descend far enough down the other side to find sufficient water for the camp.

The next several days were exhausting. But they were mixed with equal amounts of awe-inspiring wonder at the mountain peaks, still laced with snow in summer, and fear at the prospect of traveling through terrain rugged beyond anything they had experienced. However, they did draw a small amount of reassurance in the fact that it was a well-established trail covered by over ten thousand travelers before them.

Late in September, after more than three and a half months on the trail, the morning arrived as most other mornings, except for the thin layer of ice on the water bucket. They coaxed their bodies into leaving the warmth of their blankets and fanned the fire back into some flame to warm up a quick cup of cornmeal before packing up and preparing to move out. About midday as they rounded a slight bend in the road, Joseph expected to see yet another range of mountains that had to be climbed. Instead, what he and the others saw left him speechless, almost breathless. Stretched out before them lay the Great Salt Lake reflecting the midday sun. The lake was surrounded by the large valley that filled his field of view completely, right and left. A cluster of buildings and a fort were near the north end of the valley.

Ann Eliza climbed down from the wagon and stood silently next to Joseph. He took off his hat as they sank to their knees. He took her hand, and they bowed their heads, giving thanks for arriving safely and for what lay before them. It had been one of the hardest, physically grueling periods of their lives. The loss of their children had been spiritually exhausting, but this journey had helped them to work through and eventually conquer their grief as they focused on their new home and a new beginning. What lay before them was both awe-inspiringly beautiful as well as intimidating and frightening. Beautiful were the massive, rocky peaks surrounding the valley to protect them from those who would persecute, taunt, and menace them. And it was frightening, knowing those same mountains were home to wild animals and Indians who resented them being there. The mountains that would bring deep snow and bitter cold would also be stingy in allowing them to grow and stockpile food. But here in this valley, they could live and practice their beliefs and live for the eternal promises they had made in the temple before they left Nauvoo.

Spontaneously, Joseph and Ann Eliza stood up, still in awe of the valley before them. Joseph reached up, grabbed his hat, and threw it as hard as he could high into the air, letting out a celebratory whoop that was joined by the others in the company. Excitement and chatter erupted as the travelers hugged each other. Even the oxen seemed to join in the celebration as they jockeyed around in their yokes, anxious to get on with it.

CHAPTER 26

It still took the rest of the day to travel the comparatively easy road into the town. At dusk, they entered Salt Lake City. A few who had family members already in the basin and were expecting them were reunited at earlier points and diverted to their homes. The others were met by church members who had heeded Brigham Young's direction to open their homes to new arrivals for a few days' rest. This gave them some time until areas and options could be assessed and a more permanent location decided on. About half of those arriving stayed in and near the city. The others looked to areas from ten to one hundred miles farther, mostly to the north or south. A few groups of people went onto St. George to the south and Preston to the north.

This was the season of new arrivals. Since the first pioneer companies arrived in 1847, the grand migration had continued. Some of the new converts were able to make the trip soon after they joined the church. More likely, a family would have to save and prepare for several years before making the trip. Some would send part of their family to help establish a home and explore the conditions before being followed by the rest of the family. Some, like Joseph and family, would make it to Winter Quarters and then have to work and save up for several years until they were prepared to go the rest of the way. Companies would leave Winter Quarters in the spring, arriving at Salt Lake in the fall. Thus, the season for arriving companies would begin about mid-July with most companies arriving by early October.

As Joseph and his family rode into Salt Lake, they passed homes that were mostly adobe. Their eyes were wide, and little was said as they drank in the sights, sounds, and smells of their new town. The majority of the company was gathering near Temple Square, the city block that had been dedicated for their new temple, though construction had not started yet. What was there was a bowery, which was a large covered area where church meetings were held. There were also several other church buildings used for church business.

"Welcome to Salt Lake City," said a young man sticking out his hand toward Joseph, about the same age as Joseph. "My name is Bro Williams. Would you and your family like to stay at my place a few days?" Joseph hadn't anticipated what exactly might happen when they entered the city, but this was a welcome surprise.

He took the man's hand and, glancing over his shoulder for an approving look from Ann Eliza, said, "That would be very kind of you. But do you have room for seven of us?"

"I don't have a large house. Nobody here has a large house, but we can clear out an extra room with a bed," he said as he eyed the adults and children.

"After nearly four months in a wagon box and on the ground, that sounds luxurious," was Joseph's response. Bro Williams's house was about a half mile away. As they walked, they reviewed the immediate life history of each of the two families and later the backgrounds of where they came from, what their occupations had been, and their conversions and experiences in the church. Joseph's life on a whaling ship was unique among the Saints and was the point of significant conversation and stories that evening. The group found sleeping that night indoors, away from the normal night sounds they were used to, a bit unnerving at first. There were no sounds of grazing and mooing livestock, and they even missed the sounds of the night birds and the breeze blowing through the brush and leaves. After an hour, they all relaxed and enjoyed the soundest night's sleep they had in months. Bro Williams was up early, as usual, tending to livestock and doing other chores. The Godfreys woke early as well, as had become their habit, but realizing they had reached the valley, they allowed themselves to drift back to sleep for another hour.

"So what do you think you'll do as an occupation here in the valley?" asked Bro Williams during breakfast.

Joseph shook his head as he chided himself for not giving it more thought before now. "We've been focused on preparing and then traveling out here. I'll have to admit I haven't given it much thought," he replied.

"Brother Brigham says we should develop a community that is independent and doesn't have to rely on anything or anyone outside the church. After being pushed around to so many places by others, that makes a lot of sense. Most everyone farms a little and has some livestock, but for a trade or producing something that might be needed in the valley, let me make some suggestions." Brother Williams started naming off twenty ideas or more, including stone cutting, hide tanning, road building, ditch digging, and coal mining. That last one, Joseph immediately dismissed, as it would require working underground. Joseph could only see himself working outside in the weather. But another one caught his attention, and he found himself focused more and more on building a sugar-cane press and making molasses. The idea of producing something to sweeten their bland diets of the time appealed to him. Plus, cooking down the sweet juices pressed out of sugar cane into molasses was, at least somewhat, similar to cooking blubber into whale oil in the try-pots on a ship. After a couple more days and lots of discussions, Joseph loaded up his wagon and headed toward the north end of the valley. Mary and her son, Moroni, had other ideas.

"You know you're welcome to go with us," Joseph said to Mary as he started to get the oxen hitched to the wagon. "I've not changed one bit from the promise I made to George. You're always welcome in our home and at our table, both you and Moroni."

"I feel like I've burdened you long enough," was her response. "You know, I've got a sister west of the city in Tooele. She said I could stay with her. So, as you head north, I'll go west and see what happens." Joseph wasn't surprised with her decision. Mary had always felt like she stuck out like a sore thumb since being without George. She kept to herself, and even during the trek across the plains, she didn't always travel with Joseph's family, latching onto different families as they made the journey. She was grateful for all that Joseph and Ann Eliza had done, but now was a chance to go a different direction. Her sister Matilda, her husband, and their two boys had traveled to the valley the year before and had settled southwest of the city.

Joseph acquired some farm ground about forty miles north of Salt Lake City. As they left the city, everything they owned was in a wagon box, plus the two oxen that pulled the wagon. They were once again starting to build a homestead from nothing. They had been in a similar situation several times before. Now they were rich, compared to the day he and George pulled themselves out of the water of New York Harbor with absolutely nothing but their underwear. He hoped this would be the last time they would have to undertake such a task. This time, everything was meant and planned to be permanent.

Over the next several years, Joseph built his family a house, started farming, and acquired more livestock, including a milk cow, chickens, a few sheep, and a couple beef cows. There was always more to do in a day than there was time to do it. He also was planning to build a sugar-cane press. He could press not only his own sugar cane but cane from other farms nearby. This would improve their diet and give them a way to produce a commodity they could easily trade and sometimes acquire some cash for.

CHAPTER 27

"Joseph, you'd better come in here." It was the midwife who had been called in to help with the birth of their eighth child. As Joseph went to the side of Ann Eliza, the midwife said in a whisper, "She's bleeding badly. I'm afraid we might lose her." Joseph was stunned at the thought he might lose his sweetheart. He had suspected something was wrong when Ann Eliza's cries at the contractions continued much longer than those of previous childbirths. Then they took on a frantic tone, one of desperation. Then the cries grew weaker. Since arriving in the valley, Joseph and Ann Eliza had had one child. This was the second. She had given birth seven times before with no unusual problems. But the mortality rate of mothers during childbirth was high and even higher for the babies. Of the seven previous births, they had lost three.

As Joseph knelt beside her, he took her hand and kissed it. "I'm here, Ann," he softly said as he choked back the tears that came to his eyes. When he looked into her face, he saw a look he'd never seen before. Her eyes were sunken. She was looking directly at him but as if she couldn't focus, like she was looking at something across the room.

"I'm afraid I'm leaving you," she whispered, exhausted by the hours of labor and resigned to an outcome beyond her control. "I love you, Joseph. Find a mother for our children."

"I love you. Don't leave me," Joseph pleaded, but there was no response. She was gone. Joseph's sobs were interrupted by the weak cry of his new daughter. The midwife had cleaned her up quickly, swaddled her in a blanket Ann Eliza had made the previous months just for her, and handed her to Joseph, hoping to blunt the pains of losing one loved one by the addition of another. Joseph held her gently but firmly, grasping at any remaining shadow of the one he had shared his trials and triumphs with since he first saw her walking toward him, pitcher of cold water in hand, in the heat of her father's New Jersey field.

"Have the children come in," he said to the midwife. His voice squeaked, as he knew he must now instill some courage and strength in his children.

Joseph was in a fog of grief the next few days. He performed his duties outside in the yard only out of habit. When he had to do something in the house, such as feed the children, he was lost. This had always been Ann Eliza's domain, and anything and everything she did pleased him. Now, he had to do it. It was hard and painful to make himself think through what had to be done and then to do it. Gratefully, the neighbors brought in enough food so he could avoid most cooking. But milk for the baby, Matilda, was a constant—getting it, storing it, and then warming it before feeding.

The day of Ann Eliza's service, three days after her death, was clear but cold. Mary had hurriedly come from west of Salt Lake City, about sixty miles. She arrived just in time for the graveside service.

"Joseph, I'm so sorry this happened," she said, approaching and then putting her arms around him and pulling him close. Joseph reciprocated while still holding Matilda with one arm. They stood in combined grief, tears flowing freely. This was welcome, needed contact for Joseph. Even though Mary had been his responsibility since George left, she had always been aloof, accepting but never acknowledging the support received from him and Ann Eliza for six years until they reached the Salt Lake Valley. "Is this your new baby?" Mary said as she reached for the little one.

Joseph nodded and whispered, "Matilda," as he put the newborn in her arms.

"The same as my sister. Can I mother her for the rest of the service?" she said as she peeked at the baby and then took her in her arms. The bishop called to gather people and signal the start of the service.

Joseph thought his heart would stop beating at the conclusion, and they lowered the casket into the ground. No, he hoped his heart would stop beating. At that moment, he saw nothing but total despair. This had to be the low point of his entire life.

Mary brought Matilda back to Joseph and gently put her back into his arms. Then she looked directly at him, directly in his eyes, and said, "Joseph, now that we're here and settled and there has been some time to think about the last several years, I realize I've not treated you well. I was very disturbed that George was taken from me, and I blamed you. That was wrong. I'm sorry. I realize the great pains you went to, to care for me and Moroni. Thank you." They embraced once more, sharing the grief they both were feeling for the one who had died. During their embrace, Joseph felt a little hope as he replayed the words she had just spoken. He had blamed himself too for Mary not having a husband to look after her and help her across the plains. With her words, he felt that weight lifted.

Life on the frontier in the mid-1800s was more dangerous than whaling on the high seas where Joseph had spent the first decades of his life. He and Ann Eliza had lost three of their eight children, nearly half their family. A high mortality was common for this time and place. In contrast, only four sailors had died while at sea during his thirty years, one being the captain due to a sudden illness, probably a stroke or heart attack. Two were drowned when they were flipped out of the whaling boat in a rough sea. And one died of some illness he encountered while out on the town in Singapore. Several were injured during the flensing of whales when they slipped off the whale and were bitten by sharks before they could be fished out of the water, and some had bad cuts from using knives in rough seas while balancing on a whale carcass. But they were bandaged up and doctored, and they eventually recovered. They always enjoyed showing off the scars or mangled limb that was the result.

Each pregnancy was a life-and-death event for a child and the mother. It was part of the risk of raising a family—a risk that most felt compelled to take. Each child could bring great joy or great sorrow.

Ann Eliza's burial service was a turning point for Joseph. A few days after, he found he was able to have logical thoughts and organization again. But as he tried to fill both roles of father and mother for his family, he realized he would not last, and he would do a poor job of trying to be both in the process. He began looking for some household help to relieve him of much of the housework. It was customary at the time for teenage immigrants to move into another's home to provide such help. Many of these immigrants had been sent ahead of the rest of their family from Europe, to get a toehold in this new country. As he discussed his dilemma with his bishop, the bishop suggested he consider Ann Price, who had arrived several years earlier from Wales. Joseph thanked him for the suggestion and told him he wanted to think on it for now. A couple more days of trying to balance the needs of his children and still take care of the stock and other chores around the farm convinced him to get out of his comfort zone and pay a visit to the Price family.

CHAPTER 28

"Good morning. Can I help you?" said the girl. Joseph guessed she was in her late teens and that she was probably the girl he came to inquire about.

"I'm Joseph Godfrey. Is your father at home?" he stammered, uncomfortable and yet resolved to see this through.

"He's out in the barn. Let me grab a shawl, and I'll show you out," she replied. As she reached behind the door for her shawl, Joseph let out a sigh and regained a measure of composure. "I've seen you at church, Brother Godfrey. I'm so sorry about your wife." She opened the door and pointed to where her father was busy milking a cow. "Daddy, Brother Godfrey is here to see you." She turned to leave.

"Please stay, Ann. This concerns you as well." Joseph introduced himself to Brother Price and after a few pleasantries got right the point of his visit. "As you know, I've recently buried my wife." To verbalize this event almost took Joseph's breath away. He had to pause a moment, take a deep breath, and steel his mind to continue. "I'm left with five children, one a newborn, and need some help caring for them. The bishop suggested Ann may be interested in coming to keep the house. I'm finding I keep the house quite poorly." There were a few seconds of awkward silence as steam gathered around the rim of the bucket of warm milk, adding to the puffs of steam emanating from the nostrils of the cow. Ann shuffled her feet and then nodded toward her father, indicating she wanted him to do the speaking. There seemed to be no question as to the reply.

"I'm sorry, Brother Godfrey, but Ann became engaged just two days ago. I'm sure the bishop doesn't know yet. We were waiting to let some other family near St. George know before we made it public. You can see our reasoning?"

The whole visit had started out a little awkward as Joseph was greeted at the door. Then it became cordial, and now it had turned awkward again, at least for Joseph. "Of course, you're right. Well … congratulations. I wish you the best. Good-bye." Joseph tried not to stumble or run into the milking stool as he made his exit.

Once outside and down the road a few hundred feet, he relaxed and was relieved that he had accomplished this interaction, the first since Ann Eliza's death, without a major faux pas. He chided himself for not having the presence of mind to ask if they might know of someone else that would be interested. The problem was still unsolved. As he walked back, passing neighbors' houses, he reviewed in his mind each family, how many children they had, their ages, and whether they were boys or girls. He admitted to himself there was a lot he didn't know about his neighbors.

Late in the afternoon just before sundown, Joseph was in the house fixing some dinner and feeding Matilda. A knock came at the door. Before him stood Brother Price and a girl younger than Ann but similar enough in looks that he guessed she was a younger sister.

"Brother Godfrey," began the man, "this is Sarah Ann, my fifteen-year-old daughter. After your visit this morning, we were talking and thought you may be interested in having Sarah Ann help you."

There was a few moments' pause as Joseph considered this offer. He looked carefully at Sarah Ann. Brother Price continued, "Sarah Ann has been helping already at other households in the area for several years now." He paused a few more seconds and then added, "But this would be the first time there wasn't the mother in the house."

This was one of those times that one would like to take several weeks or months to make a decision. But Joseph didn't have that luxury. He knew he had to decide now. He glanced down and saw she had a small bag with her, probably all her belongings, and was prepared to stay. Was this the answer he'd been praying for? It wasn't what he had in mind. But Joseph had found that prayers were nearly always answered, but rarely as he expected them to be. He slowly, slightly nodded and then was more enthusiastic. "Perhaps we could give it a trial run," he said as a way to, at least on the surface, ease into a situation that would be somewhat foreign to Sarah Ann and completely foreign to Joseph. He opened the door wide, and Sarah Ann walked into Joseph's home.

"I'll check with you in a few days," said Brother Price as he turned and walked away.

The next week proved to be about what Sarah Ann had experienced at the other homes she had worked at. Except this time, when the men were out working, she was the grown-up in the house. The men were Joseph, William or Billy, who was sixteen, and George, who was nine. Billy had become the constant companion to Joseph, both of them realizing he was becoming a man and needed to prepare to support himself and his future family. The men had fixed up a corner of the barn where they could be out of the house. After chores were finished or in cold weather, they could discuss their current situation, such as food stocks, wood, the stock, and next year's crops. Lately, they had been discussing serious details regarding the building of a cane press. Sugar was unheard of in the area, and the sweet molasses would be in high demand.

The sleeping arrangements had to be adjusted as well. Bed space was short, a serious matter. Joseph gave up his bed to Sarah Ann and three-year-old Reuben and Matilda, the newborn. Joseph took Reuben's spot with George, and Billy did the best he could on the floor and in warm weather slept in the barn or outside.

Joseph was slowly reassembling his life from the wreck it had been right after Ann Eliza passed away. However, he still felt several pieces continue to spin out of control. He fought that feeling every day and just kept repeating in his mind, "One more day. One more day. Hold it together one more day." At the same time, he kept replaying something Mary had said at Ann Eliza's burial, "Can I mother her …" referring to Matilda during the service. And immediately, Ann Eliza's final words to Joseph replayed in this mind, "Find a mother for our children." Several times he had to walk away, walk out of the house or walk away from the boys to avoid them seeing their father break down and sob uncontrollably. At one such time, he walked into the night for an hour. Finally falling to his knees, he cried as rarely seen in a man, pouring out his grief, his anger, his questions, and pleading for some comfort. He stayed there until he was numb from the cold. But when he finally rose and turned back toward home, he felt the comfort he had been seeking.

CHAPTER 29

The next day was Sunday. After church, the bishop made his way to Joseph, shaking hands through the crowd. "I see Sarah Ann is with your family this morning," the bishop said, giving Joseph a puzzled look, realizing he had suggested Sarah Ann's older sister.

"Yes," said Joseph, "we're going to give this a try."

The bishop nodded his approval and then added, "Brother Brigham will be in the area on Tuesday. He's asked to meet with you to see how you're doing."

Joseph had met Brigham Young on several occasions going clear back to Nauvoo. Even though the church was growing by thousands each month, the president still took an active one-on-one approach to his calling. "I'd be happy to," replied Joseph.

The meeting with Brother Brigham was very cordial and unusually long for such a meeting—over an hour. "Thank you for your concern and your counsel, President. I'll move forward then," Joseph said on leaving the meeting.

Even though he had committed to following the counsel of President Young, Joseph took several days thinking about what he had committed to. The president had extended a calling to him, one Joseph had not expected or previously thought about. He was overwhelmed by the call and thought long and hard about the numerous ramifications that would result from his actions and exactly what steps he would need to take to proceed. He kept repeating over and over in his mind, "I don't want to do it, but I need to do it. So, I'm going to do it. I'll start by taking one more step." Then he would focus on the results of the task instead of what specifically might be unappealing.

"How do you feel about working here, now that you've been here awhile?" Joseph asked Sarah Ann late one night as she was feeding Matilda and getting her to bed for the night. "Be honest about it. I've appreciated your help and what you've done for my family, but I wouldn't want you stuck in a position that you're uncomfortable with."

Sarah Ann paused long enough to tuck Matilda under the covers. "I feel okay about it. I feel good. I enjoy the children and being in your house," was her reply. Joseph had been extra careful dealing with this fifteen-year-old girl, to respect her feelings and position in the household, offering gentle guidance and including ample praise as a big part of the transition. Sarah Ann noticed the respect she was receiving from Joseph as she organized and carried out her household duties, and she liked it. She hadn't been treated that way in the other homes she had been in.

"I'm going to leave tomorrow and be gone for three, maybe four days," Joseph continued. "There is some business I need to tend to." Sara Ann's eyes grew wide at the thought of having the house under her total care. "Billy will be here to take care of everything outside and to make sure you've got wood and what food you may need from the cellar and milk for the baby." There were repeated questions from the kids as to where he was going. "I can't say anything now but will explain when I return." He left before sunup the next morning and headed south.

CHAPTER 30

It was a long day's ride. The winter sun had set several hours ago. Fortunately, the weather had cooperated, and it had been fairly mild for February. Both the horse and Joseph were worn out when he entered the yard, tied up his horse near the watering trough, walked to the house, and knocked on the door. A knock on the door after dark raised more than a few eyebrows inside and resulted in several peeks out the window. Joseph backed away from the door and tried to look as unthreatening as possible. A man came to the door, barely opened it, and asked, "Can I help you?"

"I'm Joseph Godfrey. Is Mary Coleman here?"

The man looked relieved. He opened the door a bit farther and said, "I'll get her. Please step inside so I can close the door." Joseph gladly complied and started soaking up the warmth from the house.

Mary came in the room, looked a bit shocked, and approached Joseph. "Joseph!" is all she could manage to say.

"Hi, Mary. It's good to see you. I've come to talk to you about something. But I wonder if I could sit and get warmed up first? I've ridden all the way today."

Mary caught herself and apologized. "Of course. Sit here by the fire. I'll warm up something for you to eat." Mary was staying with her sister and her family. She, of course, had told them about Joseph and George and all that had happened the last fifteen years. Once they knew who he was, the house was buzzing with arrangements to make Joseph comfortable after his long ride. An older boy went out and took care of Joseph's horse, making sure he had feed and water.

Everyone relaxed, and stories were told from all sides of the room as they shared events of the past several years. Someone had asked Joseph about his life before he joined the church. That opened up several hours more of whaling adventures and misadventures. All were fascinated. When the conversation finally lagged, Mary pressed Joseph as to why he came.

"It's very late," replied Joseph, not wanting to tackle the reason for his visit at such a late hour. "I think it best to get some sleep, and we can talk first thing in the morning." A spot on the floor was made for Joseph near the fire. The warmth felt so good after a long day in the freezing temperatures.

It left Mary uncertain for the night as to why he had come. She didn't sleep much as she played out several possibilities, why he rode hard all day in winter to speak with her. The next morning, as soon as breakfast was over, Mary looked directly at Joseph and cocked her head to one side as if to say, "Okay, why are you here?" without opening her mouth.

"Mary, is there somewhere *you and I* can talk?" Joseph said, indicating he'd like some privacy. The rest of the family quickly excused themselves to do morning chores and errands, and some just made up reasons to leave the room. Joseph had played out a hundred versions of exactly what he would say when this time came. He felt it best to get right to the point. "Mary, I've come to ask you to marry me," Joseph said softly but firmly. This was one of the reasons Mary had considered in her mind the night before, so she wasn't totally unprepared for the proposal. Joseph continued, "Matilda is not doing well and needs constant care. Billy is old enough, but the other children need more than just a father. When spring comes, my time is consumed with planting and all else that goes with providing for a family." Mary listened, nodding slightly to indicate she heard what he was saying. There was nothing about love or devotion or "I need you in my life." They both knew this was not the time for such words, so soon after Ann Eliza's death. Life on the frontier was about survival first. Love would come later as they achieved the first objective. Mary knew all this and understood. But she wasn't prepared for what Joseph said next. "I plan on taking a second wife as well," he continued. "I haven't asked her yet but plan to in the next few days." This surprised Mary but didn't shock her. He was quiet, allowing Mary to absorb and consider what he had just said.

This was what the lengthy meeting with Brother Brigham was mostly about. At this time, the Mormons were openly practicing polygamy. It was a calling. Most of the time, the men were asked by their priesthood leader to enter into such a marriage. Most times the man initiated it, but occasionally a woman would offer herself to a man to become an additional wife. However it was proposed, it was ultimately approved by President Young to be a valid plural marriage. The reason for polygamy, as preached in church meetings, was God commanded it at this time. Why at this time? There were several reasons—among them, to build up a righteous people to God and give more women the opportunity of a family, to stabilize the community, and provide women on the frontier the support, safety, and security of a husband.

Joseph was not anxious to have more than one wife. He'd been aware of the practice since they left Nauvoo. And while Ann Eliza was alive, he was content and happy—the happiest he'd been his entire life. He not only had a wife whom he loved dearly; he had children to add to his happiness. They were finally settled in a place where they could practice their faith without fear of persecution, and if they worked hard, their new valley would provide a good living. But with the death of Ann Eliza, Joseph's life had entered a new phase, complicated at the moment by the challenge from Brother Brigham.

"Can I ask about the other woman?" asked Mary, indicating she was considering Joseph's proposal.

Joseph explained, "You would be considered the first wife. As you know, the first wife needs to approve an additional wife, not who it is but an additional wife. Since I haven't asked her yet, I prefer not to say who it is. But I will say she is young, younger than either of us." Because Joseph ran away from home at such an early age, his birth date was always in question. And even Joseph wasn't consistent when giving his birth date, which ranged from 1796 to 1806. If we pick the middle of that range, Joseph would be twenty years older than Mary and forty-two years older than Sarah Ann. It was a striking difference by any consideration and one that would stretch Joseph's abilities to adjust to the vast differences in likes and dislikes, demeanor, energy, tolerance, life skills, and the list goes on.

"When do you plan on returning home?" Mary asked thoughtfully.

"If I leave early in the morning, it's a long day, but I would like to be back home tomorrow night," he replied.

"I'll give you my answer tonight. And, Joseph, whatever my answer is, thank you for considering me. And thanks again for all you have done for me and my son since George died."

Joseph spent most of the day tending his horse, preparing for the long ride back the next day, and helping around the yard with the animals and chores. Mary and Joseph did spend a little additional time together scattered through the day. But Joseph understood she needed most of the day alone to contemplate his offer. It was a pleasant day for Joseph, one of his best since Ann Eliza died. Being away from home removed the pressure of those responsibilities for a time. He relaxed and enjoyed the hospitality of those whose home he was in, even with the nagging uncertainty of Mary's answer.

"Yes, I will marry you," Mary said, late in the day. They embraced but didn't kiss. Her first marriage to George and Joseph's to Ann Eliza were motivated by romantic love. That was their starting point. You could say that Mary and Joseph also loved each other, but it wasn't a romantic love. It could be in time, but not yet. However, it was a love borne out of deep respect and a desire to help each other grow, meet challenges, and have a stable life. They discussed timing, when the marriage might take place. But with more pieces of the plan still needing to occur, details would have to follow later.

As Joseph arrived back at his home, it was again after dark. He was cold, hungry, and at the limit of his physical strength. He gratefully found all well. Billy took care of his horse as Joseph ate a little soup that Sarah Ann warmed up for him. He felt pleased he had accomplished the first part of his plan, and after some much-needed rest, he would talk to Sarah Ann.

CHAPTER 31

Being at home, Joseph was in more control of the situation and picked a time when the children were in bed and Matilda had just gone to sleep, hopefully for several hours.

"Sarah Ann," Joseph softly began, "there is something I need to talk to you about." This sounded a little ominous, which it would be. Sarah Ann immediately began reviewing her actions while she had been there. She thought she was taking care of everything all right, according to his desires. She braced herself for some criticism, but she couldn't think of anything he might be unhappy with. "I like what you're doing here and appreciate your help." She relaxed a little. However, she expected the next word to be "but"; it wasn't. "And I want to ask you to marry me." In rehearsing what to say leading up to this question, Joseph realized the question said it all. It said how he felt about her work there, how she was caring for Matilda and the other children, and how he felt about her as a person. She was shocked. Her eyes grew wide, and her mouth dropped open. Joseph continued, "I've also asked another woman to marry me, and she has accepted. That's where I've been the last few days. She will be the first wife, and you'd be the second." Joseph sat still, allowing the whole concept to gel in her mind. Her eyes darted around the room. He wasn't sure if that was just her way of considering the different ramifications of what he had just asked her or if she was imagining this home as her permanent home. After a pause, he continued, "I know this is unexpected. And it will take some time for you to consider it. If you like, I would even encourage you to talk to your parents about it.

Pray about it. When I met with Brother Brigham a few weeks ago, he issued a calling that I do this, that I remarry, more than one woman."

"Brother Brigham?" she said as she finally found her voice.

"He didn't say exactly who I should ask, but with the death of Ann Eliza, he said I should remarry soon, and several. I'm to report back to him when the plan is in place." Joseph again paused to allow this additional information to be absorbed. Sarah Ann was quivering, her mind overwhelmed with his unexpected proposal. Joseph, speaking softly and slowly, tried to comfort and reassure her as much as possible. "Over the next few days, you'll undoubtedly have questions. Ask me anything you want. I've been impressed with you since the first day you arrived. And I'm confident that you should become part of our family."

That night, Sarah Ann lay on her bed with eyes wide open. When Matilda fussed several hours later, Sarah Ann rose to comfort her, having not slept a minute. As she picked her up and fed her, Sarah Ann's body rocking in the chair, she imagined, for the first time, the possibility of holding and rocking her own child. Before this, she had never dared imagine even being married, let alone having children of her own.

As a few days went by, she did have questions. She asked Joseph, "Who is the other woman? Where will she live? Does she have other children? Will this house even hold all who will be here? How do you know her? Does she live close by? How long has she been here in the basin?" And perhaps the most pointed question, "What about babies?"

To this Joseph responded, "You're young, and I'm in no hurry to have more children. We'll wait until you are ready." Again, there was no talk of love or devotion. It was being approached as an arrangement, where each party had its responsibilities. Plural marriage was viewed as abhorrent behavior by most of the country, even by most of the church members when it was first introduced. There were times Joseph felt overwhelmed at the responsibility of keeping one wife supported and happy, let alone more than one wife. In many cases, the sister wives became very close friends with each other and supported each other in the struggle of life in the wilderness. Not everyone took to polygamy, and when it didn't work out, divorce was granted quite easily. The unspoken policy was that no one should be forced to stay in a marriage they didn't want to be in. But the majority of the time, the marriages worked out. Exact numbers are not available, but according to estimates, 20 to 30 percent of the members at the time practiced polygamy.

Being somewhat satisfied with the answers Joseph gave, she asked for several days to go to her parents and discuss this with them.

When Sarah Ann visited her parents to discuss Joseph's proposal, she stayed most of a week. The hope of all parents is their daughter will meet a fine, young man who is prepared to support a wife and raise a family. When Sarah Ann told them of Joseph's proposal, it wasn't what they were hoping for or expected. And that she would be a polygamist wife was somewhat startling to them. The first evening when she arrived and informed them why she was visiting, not much was said other than them asking a few questions about Joseph's circumstances. Her parents were mostly getting used to the idea. The next morning, after a night's rest and contemplation, there were many questions.

"How have you liked being there so far?" asked Sarah Ann's mother.

"It took a few days to get used to his house, the children, and the routine—when they like breakfast, do they finish the barnyard chores before or after breakfast, and the same for lunch and dinner. What kinds of foods do they prefer and which foods they prefer that are fixed different than I'm used to."

"How do you get along with the children?" her mother continued.

"Matilda seems to be usually sick with one thing or another. She takes the most time. And when she doesn't feel good, she's quite fussy. But when she's not sick, she is delightful. Reuben is three and is becoming curious about everything around him. He's easily occupied by giving him something new to look at or play with, even a kitchen utensil like a sifter or rolling pin. Young Joseph is six and wishes he were outside most of the time. When the weather permits, he's content to play in the snow for hours, building snow shapes and snow forts. George is eight and spends about half his time outside with Joseph and Billy. The rest of the time he's inside, often helping me by entertaining the little ones or doing chores in the house, putting away dishes, sweeping the floor, stuff like that. Billy is sixteen, and he spends most all his time with

Joseph, taking care of the animals and such. They, Billy and Joseph, keep talking about a cane press. What's that, Daddy?"

"It's two big rollers made to press the juice out of sugar cane. I'm glad to hear they're talking about it. It would be good for this area and give the farmers another crop they could try." Then he asked about something Sarah Ann had said earlier. "You say Billy is sixteen? You realize, if you marry Joseph, you'll be Billy's stepmother. How will he react to that, and how do you feel about that?"

"Billy is so shy, and whenever he's in the house, Joseph is there as well. Except last week for a few days. Joseph left for three days to visit and propose to the other woman. Billy brought in the milk and some potatoes and squash from the cellar when I asked him to. Most of the time, he was outside. We said a few words at meals, but that was all. He was respectful, and he slept with George while Joseph was gone." Sarah Ann was quite shy herself. In fact, even her parents were a little surprised at how much she was talking and giving details.

"That brings up another question. What have the sleeping arrangements been while you've been there?" her mother asked.

"Joseph gave up the bed he was sleeping in with Ann Eliza. Reuben, who is three, and I sleep there. Matilda has a small crib. Joseph sleeps with young Joseph and George. Billy sleeps on the floor in the corner or out in the barn when it's warm enough. He says he'll start sleeping outside in the spring."

"Have you talked to Joseph about having children?" her mother asked.

Followed immediately by her father saying, "You're so young."

"Joseph said he was in no hurry, and I would decide when I was ready to try to become pregnant."

Sarah Ann enjoyed the rest of the week being home with her parents and siblings, especially her older sister Ann, who was making her own wedding plans.

As Sarah Ann prepared to return to Joseph's house, her father indicated he would like her and her mother to sit at the kitchen table. "You're very young to be married," her father finally said, "and Joseph is a lot older than you. He's older than I am. But that could be an advantage. His farm is established, and he's considering expanding with this sugar press idea. He knows what it takes to take care of a wife and children. Sarah Ann, with all things considered, living here in this community, here in the mountains, this may be your only chance to have a husband and a family and a home of your own. That's how your mother and I feel about it, but the decision is yours."

When she returned to Joseph's, it had been nearly three weeks since Joseph had first asked her.

"I will marry you," was Sarah Ann's answer on her return from her parents. That launched a list of other arrangements Joseph needed to accomplish. One of the first items on the list was to talk to the children and explain the new arrangement to them. The younger children accepted it without question. They had grown to like Sarah Ann. Only Billy knew Mary and her son, Moroni, thirteen, who would be coming to live with them. For most of his younger years, Mary and Moroni were living near or traveling with his family. So the new arrangement wouldn't be too different from then. However, having Sarah Ann marry Joseph caused Billy some anxiety. He was sixteen, and Sarah Ann was only fifteen. He had gotten along fine with her the short time she had been in the house. But now she would be his stepmother, his father's wife, not merely a housekeeper. He was glad to hear that Moroni would be coming to live with them. The two boys were similar in age and had crossed the plains together. Having a playmate on the plains as well as someone to share chores with helped relieve the daily boredom while they were traveling.

They also needed more room. There would be nine of them in the house. Joseph started plans for adding two more rooms. The weather would soon be getting warmer, and the two older boys could sleep in the barn. At the end of one weary day of planning and arranging, Joseph thought to himself, *Brother Brigham was right in issuing this call. It has kept me so busy; I haven't had time to long for Ann Eliza. Rather, I feel I have her blessing in this. Were not her last words "find a mother for our children"?*

CHAPTER 32

March 7 was picked as the date for the marriage. Matilda was still doing poorly, and she was too little and sickly to risk taking her. Joseph had asked his closest neighbor and wife who were down the road about a quarter mile to care for her while they were gone. Billy was confident he was up to the task of caring for the others. Joseph had also alerted the bishop they would be gone. The bishop promised to have someone check on Billy and the other children. Joseph and Sarah Ann left five days before in a wagon with a few clothes and provisions. By wagon, it took two days to Mary's, a day to pack her and Moroni's belongings, and a day back to Salt Lake, arriving late in the day. President Brigham Young himself performed the marriage the next day. Then it was another day's travel back to Joseph's home north of Salt Lake. The travel wasn't pleasant. The winter had eased up a little, but that meant mud and frequent rain showers. When they finally arrived back home, all were exhausted, muddy, wet, and anxious to rest up and get cleaned up. The extra rooms to the house had only just been started, so with the additional people, all were cramped and did whatever they could to find a modest space to live in.

After a good, dry night's rest, Joseph called everyone together for a family meeting. He introduced everyone and gave a little life history of each, except Mary and Sarah Ann. Then he asked Mary and Sarah Ann to give their own introductions and brief histories. The additional rooms became the priority. Joseph, Billy, George, and now Moroni worked constantly, and in several weeks the family expanded into the added rooms. It was a big improvement, but it was still close quarters, closer than most would prefer.

By then, the spring work and planting had started, which flowed into summer, and then into fall and the harvest season and preparing for winter. Through all this time, when the men had spare time, they worked to build the cane press. All looked forward to having the sweet molasses to make candy and for special occasions. The pressed cane stocks could be used as additional high-energy feed for the cattle, sheep, and goats. Sugar cane grows best in warmer, more humid climates. A few immigrants who were from warmer climates were familiar with growing and pressing sugar cane. They realized that in the frigid mountain valleys, the production wouldn't be nearly as good. But at this point, they had nothing to use as a sweetener, and they were willing to try most anything.

The first step in raising sugar cane was to locate some starts. Joseph knew sugar cane was already being grown in areas south of Salt Lake City. The next spring, he loaded up the two older boys in the wagon and made a trip to see if he could acquire some starts. Farming in the Great Basin was a new experience. It was a lot of trial and error in discovering what crops would grow. Joseph learned that like potatoes, sugar cane grew not from seeds but from cane saved from the year before, cut into smaller pieces and then planted. When harvested, the cane, like potatoes, had to be kept from freezing to be viable to plant the next spring. Just like a barn was needed to protect the animals, a root cellar was needed deep enough in the ground to keep from freezing. The cellar was used to store not only potatoes and sugar cane but all their fruits and vegetables. Not being raised on a farm meant years of learning from those who had.

Building a press to extract the juice would be a challenge. Joseph was not very mechanical, mostly because he hadn't been exposed to much machinery, if any. While on their trip to get some cane starts, they looked long and hard at the press that was being used. Billy even made a sketch of what they saw, with notes to help them remember how it was made and how it worked.

"Well, boys," Joseph said as they were making their way back home, "do you think we can do this, or are we just chasing a fairy tale?" Joseph had adjusted to working with Billy and Moroni and thoroughly enjoyed tackling challenges together. At first it was a little rough because he found that the three of them were very different—their likes and dislikes, how they would approach a challenge, and how they responded to the tedious, day-after-day chores and other farm work. Joseph had learned to use those differences in a positive way. He allowed and encouraged each boy to pursue tasks in his way. Billy's approach was more pen and paper. He loved reading and learning and soaked up everything he could find to read. There wasn't much available to read in the area other than the scriptures, which always had a prominent place in the house. Moroni took after his mother; he was very independent and was always looking for a different way to achieve the results he wanted. Billy's sketch of the cane press was a good idea; it hadn't been thought of by the other two and became quite valuable as they constructed the press. Moroni added several changes to the design from what they had seen, which he felt would improve the effectiveness of the press.

As the family was bigger now and was growing, Joseph was looking for a way to expand his farming operation. He saw a cane press as a way to do that and to provide additional work for his boys. George was now old enough to help and needed to be kept busy. Operating the press would take at least two men, plus a man to watch the boiling of the juice. Care had to be taken to keep the fire stoked with wood—but not too much so as to scorch the juice. It also had to be frequently skimmed, which would remove additional impurities and keep it from forming clumps. After they had the operation developed, they would encourage neighboring farmers to grow sugar cane as well. They found that the cane could be harvested, cleaned, cut, and stacked in large stacks. Then later it was hauled to the press. By doing this, they could keep the press operating continually for several months. Joseph would take a share of the neighbors' molasses as payment. Sweet molasses was always in demand and was easy to sell or trade for other commodities.

CHAPTER 33

"I was at the store to pick up some rope and another scythe today, and the postman asked me to bring this letter to you," Joseph said to Mary as he came in for dinner. Letters were rare, so this got everyone's attention.

"It must be a mistake," she said as she took the letter and eyed it carefully, turning it over and over. "I can't even think of anyone who would possibly send me a letter. It's from New York. Now I'm very puzzled."

"It's addressed to Mary Coleman," Joseph added. "The postman said he thought you had been a Coleman before we got married. You are the only person he could think of that it might be for."

Mary opened the envelope containing several documents. As she read, a whole range of emotions played out across her face. It was hard, but all in the room kept quiet and allowed Mary to continue reading. "My brother passed away," she finally said softly. This brought more silence, and then condolences were offered by several in the group as they filtered away. Seconds before, all were excited by the arrival of a letter. Now the mood reversed. "I didn't even know he was in New York," she said to Joseph, being the only one left to comfort her at this bad news. "He left me some money."

Joseph had known Mary's brother Rueben when he worked on her father's farm in New Jersey. Mary and Ann Eliza were teens when he was born, and he became their favorite little brother. As he grew, his relationship with his father became strained, as Rueben didn't care for farm work as the other boys in the family. Instead, he preferred art and music and often threatened to leave the farm and find work in the

128

city, where such inclinations could be pursued and developed. Joseph and Mary were now seated at the table as they continued to review the documents contained in the envelope and reminisce about the days on the farm and what may have happened after Mary and Ann Eliza left. As Mary reviewed the death certificate, she let out a faint gasp. "He died several years ago," she said quietly to explain her surprise. As she reviewed more documents, she was able to piece together a probable chain of events. She continued, "It appears he left the farm several years after we left. He found work in New York and got a job in a theater. He was good at it and after a few years was making more than he needed to live on. So he started a bank account and started saving the extra money. When he opened the account at the bank, he named Ann Eliza and me as co-owners and beneficiaries of the account. He didn't know exactly where we were or would be, so he listed our address only as 'Out West with the Mormons.' An attorney tracked us down as living in Nauvoo, then Winter Quarters in Nebraska, and finally Salt Lake City. The church then found me here married to you on the church records. He never married." She didn't say how much money Rueben had left her. Joseph never asked. He simply reasoned she would save the money for some future purpose.

Several months later, the second little daughter of Mary and Joseph had been born, and one boy had been born to Sarah Ann and Joseph. But Matilda, the last child of Joseph and Ann Eliza, had died. Four of the eight children of Joseph and Ann Eliza had died.

The house was going from crowded to very crowded. The cane press was starting to operate, and, as typical with new operations, many long hours were being required to hammer out the bugs and learn how to set the equipment to get the most efficiency. Joseph was very aware of the conditions at the house, and he had mentally made a commitment that he would address the problem of more room as soon as he and the boys got the press running smoothly. It was a topic of discussion almost every night at dinner, right behind how the press operation was improving a little each day. However, on this particular evening, Mary was unusually quiet and seemed a little anxious about something. Finally, when the children were in bed and the babies settled for the night, Joseph asked Mary directly what was bothering her.

"I've bought a house," she replied firmly, with a little defiance in her voice. Joseph's mouth dropped open as he started to respond, and then he wasn't sure just what to say or ask first. Mary anticipated some of the questions and continued, "It's the Roberts' house, the one that's been empty about a quarter mile east of here. Moroni and I have packed our things and will use the wagon and move there tonight. We'll leave the two girls asleep here tonight, and we'll be back in the morning for breakfast and to pick them up. Sarah Ann has agreed to watch them tonight should they need any attention." Having said that, Mary relaxed a little and sat down. Joseph, still stunned, had not gotten a word out. After a short pause and taking a few deep breaths, Mary continued, "Remember the money my brother left me? That's what I used to buy the house." She anticipated Joseph's first question would be why, so she continued. "Joseph, we all know we're out of room. You've been so busy with the harvest and starting the press and church callings. I saw an opportunity to fix what was becoming a big problem. And rather than expend more time and energy discussing it from every angle, I just did it. And we're moving tonight."

On one hand, Joseph wanted to be upset at her for doing all this without talking to him. She had talked to Sarah Ann, Billy, and Moroni to get their help in arranging the move, and none of them had said anything to Joseph. On the other hand, she had solved a looming problem for Joseph. Mary's independent streak was still apparent, a streak that was evident back before Mary and George had married. At the time, Joseph felt she was just trying to distinguish herself as different from Ann Eliza, and not just another Reeves girl. But after nearly twenty years, Joseph had to acknowledge it was more than that. It was part of her character. Now, both families would have some much-needed space. Mary had thought it out carefully, anticipating the questions and objections Joseph would have. In the end, Joseph simply nodded his head and said, "Thank you, Mary," as he wrapped his arms around her and then helped to load the wagon.

CHAPTER 34

The day-to-day duties and responsibilities hadn't changed much for Sarah Ann after the marriage. There was still the washing, cooking, cleaning, and raising children. Now there were more people in the house. Until Mary moved out, they had divided up the chores. Joseph was true to his word that they would wait until she felt she was ready, eighteen, before becoming pregnant. Sarah Ann had always been a quiet girl, but after the baby was born, she became increasingly withdrawn. Some days she hardly got out of bed. Joseph, thinking she must have the flu or a bad cold, picked up some of the household chores.

One day while at the store, he ran into Sarah Ann's father and told him that she wasn't feeling well. He confided to Joseph that it sounded like depression, severe depression, and that it was a trait that ran in his family. When the word got around that she struggled with depression, everyone seemed to have a pet cure. Thus began years of trying countless remedies, of dutifully living exacting, detailed, consistent routines, of consuming countless bottles of potions and bushels of herbs, and even invoking the power of God in numerous blessings, prayers, and fastings. At times, Joseph could see on her face and in her stature that she was in pain, a mental agony that few people could understand except by living with her. The illness seemed to cycle. Months could go by that seemed lost to her. On the other side of the cycle, Sarah Ann was happy and enjoyed being a mother, homemaker, and wife. After several years, the only pattern apparent was that she seemed to feel better while she was pregnant. There must be some change in her blood or mind relating to the pregnancy that seemed to alleviate much of the despair she often felt.

"Joseph, why do I feel this way?" she asked him one evening after a long period of mental darkness. "I'm not worried about anything particular. My life is full of good things. I have a loving husband, a home, a family. We have enough food and clothes. I can't point to any reason I should feel so low."

"Everybody suffers some degree of depression at times in their life," Joseph responded. The house was quiet, and they were the only ones still awake. "Any depression should not be taken lightly. But most of the time, depressive periods are temporary and will pass. I know you feel exhausted. Exhausted not only from enduring the depression but from trying countless solutions. Some people are born with a birth mark or a bad heart. Some men go bald. To some degree, we all have to learn to live with this imperfect, mortal body. Your depression is a trait that is inherited. It's not a punishment. Don't feel that way. Like all illness, it must be something we have to go through as a learning experience."

"I haven't discovered what I'm supposed to learn yet," Sarah Ann said, feeling a tiny bit better this evening. "This depression keeps reoccurring. I feel like I'm tiptoeing along a crumbling edge, barely able to keep enough footing to avoid being sucked into the blackness, while not caring if I am pulled into that vacuum where there is no air. If my body hadn't, of its own, assumed the responsibility to draw breath, I would have felt the effort was not worth the reward or responsibility to continue living."

Joseph had learned several important, key things about serious depression. The fact that Sarah Ann was talking as much as she was was a sign she felt a little better, even though she wouldn't recognize any improvement in herself. When depressed, any amount of talking or conversing took a major effort. Conversing was hard because it required effort to follow a line of logic, keep track of what the other person said, and formulate a response. She would often sleep twelve to fourteen hours at a time. In the daytime, she would simply lie on her bed in a dark room or sit on a chair in a corner, not interacting with anyone. Joseph also learned that one of the symptoms of depression is that it discourages the person from doing anything that might help them feel better. One of the most common bits of advice is to get outside, go for a walk, or get some exercise. She didn't care. Even if she logically knew it would help, she couldn't make herself do it. It required too much effort. Joseph would have to oversee any herbs or medicine she might be taking. He would have to give it to her and watch her take it. Not that she would resist, but to remember how much and when to take it required more effort than she could muster. Dark clouds were all around her. She had tunnel vision because she had no interest outside a narrow tunnel of sight directly in front of her.

"Do you suppose Christ felt depressed when he was suffering in the Garden of Gethsemane?" Sarah Ann asked Joseph.

"I've never thought about it that way. I know he suffered more than we can understand," Joseph said.

"Every time I reread in the Bible about his suffering, I see it has all the elements of extreme depression. It says he was very heavy, so much so that he wished for death. Even an angel sent to buoy him up seemed to bring no improvement. I often wish for death. It looks like the light at the end of the tunnel. It beckons to me. It promises relief from this agony. It's a fight not to give in, an exhausting fight."

At this, Joseph's eyes grew wide, and his eyebrows raised as he asked, "Have you considered ending your life?"

"Many times," she answered quickly. Then after a long pause, she said, "What has kept me from following through is I look at you and the children and know how hurt you and they would be. I don't want to hurt anybody. Ending my life would be like transferring the pain I feel onto my family. I don't want that. That's what keeps me from acting on that urge."

CHAPTER 35

"Mamma, how are we going to get seventy-five candles on Daddy's birthday cake?" asked six-year-old David. The family had been preparing for several days for Joseph's birthday dinner.

"We're not exactly sure he will be seventy-five," answered Mary. "We just know it's his birthday, and he'll be *about* seventy-five. So we'll just make his favorite cake with his favorite frosting and sing 'Happy Birthday' to him."

David was Mary's youngest, but Sarah Ann was still nursing the family's newest arrival, Josiah. The family continued to grow. Several of the older children had married and moved out but were planning on being part of the birthday festivities. Even though the family was living in two houses, Sarah Ann's house had the largest room to accommodate the family for the event. And even then, many spilled into other rooms and the yard before and after the meal.

To cap off the celebration, Mary and Sarah Ann had planned a time after the meal when Joseph could say a few words to all who had gathered. Sarah Ann had emphasized the word "few" several times to Joseph when she asked him to say a few remarks.

"The younger kids will be antsy and anxious to be off playing," Sarah Ann said, justifying her request to keep his remarks short.

The meal was excellent. The family enjoyed each other. The conversation ranged from the prospects of Utah becoming a US state to how the cane-press operation was progressing on this year's sugar cane crop to the newest fashions brought in by the latest travelers through the area now that the railroad ran through the valley. After "Happy

Birthday" had been sung and the cake cut and distributed, Mary tried to bring quiet to the group for a few words from Joseph. About the time the clamor subsided so Joseph could be heard, Josiah wanted to be fed and started a fuss that could not be ignored.

"I'll take him in the other room and feed him so you can continue," Sarah Ann said as she gathered him up and made her way into the other room.

About the newest addition, Joseph quipped, "I understand heaven is quite crowded right now." The room quieted to hear the punch line. "Because the Lord keeps trying to make more room by sending babies to our house." The room erupted into laughter. "And I'm glad he does, so I'll be sure to have someone to milk Bessie when I get too old." More laughter. "I've been told to keep it short, so I have just two things to say. The first thing is the best birthday present I could have is having you all here to share it with me," he said in a firm, serious tone that let everyone know it was said from the heart. "And the second thing I want to say is, considering where I started as a boy, all the tough times, the sorrow and the despair it took to get here, it's worth it, and I would do it all again." His words were thoughtful and said with such meaning that even though his remarks were over, the group seemed to pause for a few minutes to respect what he had said and let it sink a little deeper.

Naturally, the younger kids, anxious to start their games, stirred first and pulled on their coats, caps, and mittens to go outside to play in some of the remaining snow. The winter had been long and cold. But this was March, and the snowdrifts were now slowly giving away to the next season of the year, mud. Most people called it spring. But for farmers, it was the season that gave them the itch to start projects and be in the fields plowing and planting, but the mud just wouldn't let them for a couple more months.

The kids who had gone outside to play now came charging back into the house, scared and excited. "Indians! Indians are outside, Daddy! They're by the barn."

"It's okay, kids. Settle down. I'll go talk to them," Joseph reassured the group. "Billy, let's go see what they want." The two men put on their coats, being calm but deliberate to send the message to all that the situation shouldn't worry them. Indians showing up like this was not uncommon, and usually the occurrence ended with the exchange of some information and some food given to the Indians. It was a nonevent. But sometimes they showed up because they were angry or upset about something and wanted revenge or some restitution.

Walking out toward the barn, Joseph took strides that were longer and more definite than usual, showing his visitors he was confident and unafraid. Billy walked almost shoulder to shoulder with him but didn't show the same level of confidence. As they approached the small group of Indians, Joseph recognized the brave as one who had occasionally visited him before. He went by the name of Benny, an English name that sounded similar to his Native American name but was easier for the settlers to pronounce and remember. With Benny was his squaw, Joseph assumed, and a toddler huddled in the folds of her skirt. While still fifteen to twenty feet away, Joseph raised his hand in a sign of greeting while lifting his head slightly. Benny did the same.

"Welcome, Benny," Joseph said as he stood within a few feet, looking directly into the eyes of the brave while being careful not to look at the squaw or child. But in his peripheral vision he could see both were in poor condition, and the child was shaking with cold.

"Greetings, Emigary," Benny responded. The title "Emigary" was one that had to be earned and meant "trusted friend," a high title only occasionally given by the Indians. "The winter too long. Squaw and Papoose have no meat," Then Benny glanced down at the child and added, "Are cold." Even though he never mentioned himself, Joseph could tell he was as cold and hungry as they were and was probably there on the insistence of the squaw.

Joseph waited what seemed like an hour to Billy but was only a few seconds. Then, with only a hint of a smile, he responded, "All my family are here. We have just finished our meal. We have some extra. Come to the house while we fix it for you." Joseph stepped so he was directly between Benny and Billy. Facing Billy, he said softly, "I wouldn't bring them into the house with the little kids there, but they're so cold. Send the little ones into another room. Ask Mary to wrap up the leftovers. I'll be a bit slow bringing them to the house."

Billy walked briskly to the house and did as Joseph had asked. He spoke calmly but firmly in an unhurried voice, not wanting to raise undue anxiety, especially in the children. When Joseph and the Indians walked into the house, the warmth of the house and smell of the meal overwhelmed their senses, and their eyes darted uncontrollably to the stove where Mary was wrapping up some food. They unconsciously licked their lips as their mouths began to water. The stoic adults stood as if at attention while the youngster shuffled back and forth in anticipation of the food. Mary, realizing they were extremely cold and were basking in the warmth of the house, purposely dragged out the chore she was doing, giving them a few more minutes of warmth. When Mary finished wrapping the food, she didn't give it to Benny. She handed it to Joseph, who then handed it to Benny.

"Be strong, my friend," Joseph said as he handed the food to Benny.

"Thank you, Emigary," said Benny as he nodded to Joseph. The nod was a rare show of a measure of respect and gratitude. Benny put the package under his thin coat and spun around to make his exit. The squaw, in an even rarer show of emotion, looked directly into Joseph's eyes, and with her eyes moist, she silently mouthed the words, "Thank you." The Indians quickly moved out of sight before they ate any of the food.

Joseph sat down at the table, breathed an audible sigh of relief, and let his shoulders slump as the tension began to leave his body. Several of the older family members sat down around the table as well.

"Were you scared, Joseph?" Mary asked after a few seconds.

"No, but you never know." Joseph took another deep breath and then said, "You just never know what kind of greeting and response you'll get. You always have to be mentally prepared for a negative encounter." There was another pause. Then he added, "A few things to always remember—be bold and confident in your communication. Only be confrontational as a last resort. And always show the proper respect to them and to others who may be with you." He didn't say it, but Joseph felt the encounter was good for the whole family to see how such an unexpected event was managed. He also felt this meeting would influence, in a positive way, any future meetings with Benny.

CHAPTER 36

Joseph stood up slowly from milking the cow. The fact was he probably wouldn't have made it up had he not used the cow's tail to help steady himself and pull himself up. "Thanks, Bessie," he muttered to the old cow, who in her younger days would have filled the bucket to overflowing. But lately, about one-third of a bucket was the best she could do. "You know, Bessie, I'm glad you don't give as much milk as you used to. It's easier to carry to the house. I'm not as tough as I used to be." He stroked her back a few times as he made sure she had enough grain.

The nights were getting colder now. It would be Christmas in a few weeks. Joseph remembered when Bessie was born, close to fifteen years ago now. Back then, it was just Bess. Bessie knew the innermost thoughts of Joseph's heart. When no one else would listen or care, Bessie listened to his outlandish ideas, his frustrations, and his questions about life, religion, and wives. She was even the recipient of the occasional outpouring of gratitude for a life that started out quite rocky. But some would say it was nothing less than a miracle to be where he found himself at this point—which, he concluded, was near the end. He was eighty, give or take a few years. He wasn't exactly sure how old he was. Last Sunday's lesson in church was about Abraham, Sariah, and Isaac. Joseph found himself comparing his family to that of Abraham. Sariah conceived Isaac when she was about eighty years old, according to Bible scholars. Abraham would have been close to ninety years old. Sariah laughed out loud, according to the Bible, when she was told she would yet have a son at her age.

Three wives and twenty, or was it twenty-two, children had blessed Joseph's life. He wasn't sure of the exact number. Four children in the last ten years, with the newest just last month. He shook his head and marveled at the thought of his newborn, at his age. But Sarah Ann was just thirty-eight, still in her prime.

"It hasn't all been easy, Bessie." He continued to stroke her neck as he reminisced. Running away from home when he was just seven to escape the beatings inflicted on him by his father was overshadowed by words that had been seared in his mind: "This is the captain of this ship. You, sir, on shore, looking for your son, Joseph. He is with us, and he will stay with us. We have seen the wounds and abuse you have inflicted on him. *You will never see your son again!*" Joseph always remembered that first kindness shown him by a stranger. And for the next several decades, the captain taught and guided Joseph and helped him develop the character he needed for what was to follow. Bessie was the only witness to the tears frequently shed as Joseph gave thanks for the richness of his life. If he could have seen the end from the beginning, he simply would not have comprehended the grandeur he now felt.

The night was clear and crisp. As Joseph carried his part bucket of milk back to the house, he stopped and looked up at the celestial show emerging above the soft but brilliant glow near the western horizon. "It has been a beautiful day, turning into a beautiful night," he marveled. "I could not be more blessed." Seconds later, he clutched his chest and fell to his knees, spilling the milk.

NOTES

In the effort to sift through and collect various names, dates, and facts of our ancestors' lives, it's easy to overlook that they had thoughts, feelings, and ideas that are essential to who they really were and what kind of personalities and relationships existed. This book attempts to show a more intimate side of these great people and is the product of the author. However, I am grateful for all the research and compilation previously done and have drawn on events from the following sources to create this story:

Joseph Godfrey, a compilation of various sources, compiled and edited by Ellen Claire Weaver Shaeffer, 2008.

The Coleman-Godfrey Family History by Patricia Sessions.

The History of George Coleman and Joseph Godfrey by Laverne Coleman Akroyd.

The Coleman Book.

The Life of Joseph Godfrey and Sarah Ann Price Godfrey by Theresa Chadwick Lowder.

Biographical Sketch of Joseph Godfrey by John W Gibson, 1935.

Joseph Godfrey, told by Mary Ellen Godfrey Meacham.

A Brief Sketch of the Life of Joseph Godfrey by J. Arthur Meacham.

https://history.lds.org/overlandtravels.

https://byustudies.byu.edu/, Journal of Thomas Bullock, edited by Gregory R. Knight.

https://archive.org/details/williamclaytonsj00clay, published by the Clayton Family Association.

JOSEPH GODFREY

Joseph Godfrey was born about 1800 near Bristol, England. At seven years old, he was left to care for the house and a younger sister while his alcoholic father worked in the shipyards carrying freight on and off ships. The father, returning home drunk at night, often beat Joseph. After an unusually bad beating, Joseph determined to run away and take his chances on his own. He became a stowaway on a whaling ship and spent the next thirty years growing and maturing under the care of a kind captain. Events pushed Joseph and a friend, George Coleman, to leave the ship while in New York Harbor. The alcoholic father and adventures at sea proved only to be a prelude for the rest of his life, which would take him across the American frontier, settling and raising his family in the Rocky Mountains.

ABOUT THE AUTHOR

Linden Fielding was raised in the western United States on a large family farm. He received a degree at Utah State University in agricultural and irrigation engineering. He married Ann Godfrey, and they raised their family of five children on the farm. After raising their family, he became general manager of an international construction company, traveling and conducting business in many countries of the Middle East, Europe, Asia, the Orient, and most states of the United States. Retired, he has devoted significant time to researching the lives of notable ancestors, learning the details of their daily struggles. Going beyond names and dates greatly enhances the appreciation of these men and women and what they experienced.

CPSIA information can be obtained
at www.ICGtesting.com
Printed in the USA
FSOW01n2224031215
14182FS